Stories Told *by* Traveling Salesmen

Alan M. Oberdeck

Copyright © 2021 by Alan M Oberdeck

All rights reserved. This book or any portion thereof may not be reproduced or used in any manner whatsoever without the express written permission of the publisher except for the use of brief quotation in a book review.

Inquiries and Book Orders should be addressed to:

Great Writers Media
Email: info@greatwritersmedia.com
Phone: (302) 918-5570
24A Trolley Square #1580 Wilmington, DE 19806-3334, USA

ISBN: 978-1-960939-96-8 (sc)
ISBN: 978-1-960939-97-5 (eb)

Table of Contents

Introduction vii
    The CB Radio 1
    Breaker, Breaker 8
    The Day of Change 24
    The Trip to Memphis 33
    The Bar Fight in Tennessee 39
    Airplane Flu 43
    The Divorced Salesman 49
    The DON 63
    The Comeuppance 69
    Fred and Ella 75

The People We Meet
    Encounter 79
    The Father's Son 93
    The Right Seat in the Car 98
    The Social Circle Affair 107
    North Little Rock Motel 124
    Lost Baggage 128
    Magic Forest 133
    Prescience 138

The Danger Associated with Travel
    The Coffin Trip 144
    Requiem 153
    Witch Hazel's Broom 160
    One Chinaman 169

Other Stories
    Eine Coke bitte!.. 173
    The Interview 176
    The Performance 183
    Tom 189
    Pondering Time! 191

Introduction

What is a knight anyway? There were knights-errant from the days of chivalry. Some men pledged their fighting abilities to the service of a king or country, men who chose to defend all those who depended upon the positive outcome of some struggle. Usually, they rode warhorses and wore armor to protect themselves from their enemies. Some have likened them to armored tank drivers.

There is this popular conception of this armored man with his horse, his squire, his sword, his lance, and his mace riding off into the Arthurian landscape in search of adventure. This was usually defined as the righting of wrongs, the upholding of the truth and the never-ending search for the Holy Grail. In Arthur's day, this was all done in the name of the king.

As the twentieth century began to unfold, the fond memories of chivalry began to blur and a new group of people were lovingly and jokingly referred to as *knights of the road*. These fellows were the bums, drifters, hobos, etc.

The stories in this book are dedicated to another group of men and women. These brave souls roam the world in the employ of a *"king"* which is generally known as a company or corporation, armed with sword and lance (pen and pencil), on a valiant steed (by company car or on public airplanes), with office backup as the only squire. These valiant people go forth to battle battalions of purchasing agents and each other, to uphold the truth, right the wrongs, and search forever for the Holy Grail (the big order).

These knights are known as Sales Engineers, Salesmen, Saleswomen, Sales Managers, District Managers, or simply Traveling Salesmen. They are as dedicated as the glamorous knights of old, leaving their home and their family to go alone into the *jaws of the enemy* to do battle.

These stories can be categorized into six categories. The reality of travel.

1. The people we work with.
2. The people we meet.
3. The supernatural or Science fiction
4. The danger associated with travel.
5. Other stories

Many of these stories will have elements of several groups embedded in them, and it will be up to you as to which category would best fit them.

The purpose of this book is not to train the reader to be a salesman, nor to tempt them to join this life of toil, but to solely entertain them. You who sell may appreciate a few stories written with the salesman as the main character; we who sell seldom see this unless we are watching a sales training film. But you, who are not in sales, are to be entertained and introduced to another pattern of thought which may broaden your perspective.

Sincerely,
Alan M. Oberdeck
Traveling Salesman (*Ret.*)

The CB Radio

There was a time when traveling salesmen were less encumbered by rules and regulations. We didn't have cellphones, we couldn't be tracked by satellite, and our expenses weren't as tightly scrutinized by the IRS. Truly, it was a different time. So, what does this have to do with the CB radio?

An abbreviated history of the Citizens Band Radio, CB for short, goes back to 1945. After WWII, when things began to come back from the war footing, there was a push for more private citizens to get on the *Public Air Ways*. There was already a way for a person to be licensed and to broadcast on the air, but that was to become a short-wave radio station. This was referred to as *Amateur Radio Service*.

Many countries recognized a need for this and created similar services. As with all things controlled by the Federal Government, this was a lengthy and expensive procedure. You were required to pass a stringent test, which included working with the morse code. You were also required to have a base station, and what you could do was limited to talking to other operators.

These operators were often referred to as "Ham" operators. These Ham stations worked well during emergencies as they could communicate with other Ham stations and get out the news of what was happening. This, however, was not practical for the average citizen. Therefore, after the war, the government took a number of frequencies used by the Amateur Radio Service. And in September

1958, they created the Citizens Band with 23 channels for the CB Radio system.

In 1977, because of the popularity of the system, they expanded it to 40 channels. There were limitations on the power distribution of the signal. In the early days, they limit the power to 3.8 watts, but then raised it to 4 watts later on.

Usually, the CB radios were used by local businesses to communicate with their employees who were working away from their place of business. As there were no cell phones and finding a pay phone wasted a lot of time, the CB became a very useful thing for a business to have. The range on a good day could be up to 5 miles which usually covered the working area for most businesses. This usage remained pretty constant up until the 1970s. Many *over-the-road* trucks were owned by *Owner Operators*, either leased to a freight company, or working on contract hauls. In these cases, the CB became a very useful tool for them also. A trucker hauling in an unfamiliar area could call and ask directions to truck stops, and in case of an emergency, for help from other truckers. Many times, a trucker would ask other truckers for directions to the company he was delivering a load to. Most Owner Operators had a base station set up in their homes.

This base station also allowed the wife access to the airwaves. It was known that in a state of an emergency, a trucker talking to other truckers could get a message passed hundreds of miles back to his home base. It was also known to happen that a wife would be able to contact her husband through this informal trucker's network. Truckers never used their legal name when talking on the CB. They would adopt some descriptive name when signing on or off the air. These names were referred to as the trucker's *"handle"*. A few of them that I remember were Daddy Rabbit, Harry Houdini, Bionic Watermelon, Casanova, The Left Wheel, Bugs Bunny, Sweet Pea, Snow White, and the Mechanic.

I think that *CB-ers* had a lot of fun *choosing* their handles. Before 1972, there weren't many four-wheelers on the road talking on the radio. At that time, most of the truckers used channel 19.

During those days, channel 9 was designated as the Emergency Channel and was usually kept clear of any nonemergency chatter. Often, the truckers would monitor the traffic on channel 9 just to see what was happening.

There were two things that brought about the drastic change in CB usage. The first one was the oil embargo of 1973. And the second one was the lowering of the National highway speed limit to 55 miles per hour by the Carter administration. This was referred to as the "Double Nickel" by the truckers, and later, to all who traveled using the CB. Before that, many truckers were able to move at the speed limit posted in each state; that was usually 65 to 70 miles per hour.

Most truckers were also paid by the mileage they drove. There was also no limit to the hours they could drive in a day. At a speed limit of 65 miles per hour, a trucker could cover a good 575 to 600 miles in a day. At 0.31USD a mile, they could make 178.25 to 186.00 dollars a day.

With the speed limit dropped to 55 miles per hour, they could only travel 500 miles on a good day; that would lower their income to 155 dollars a day, which was a 16.7% pay cut that most truckers would found hard to absorb. This, along with the increased price of fuel, had the drivers in the trucking industry in a mild rebellion. The answer was to "speed". But the state's answer to "speeding" was to issue speeding tickets.

The average road salesman faced the same problem. With the reduced speed limit, his ability to make the same number of contacts in each day suffered. His answer was longer days, and instead of working in the office on Fridays, he was now spending Fridays on the road and Saturdays in his office doing his reports.

The trucker's response to this was to talk to each other on the CB to find out where the State Patrol or the local police had set up radar traps. The State Patrol officers manning these traps were generally referred to as *"Smokies"*, as their hats usually resembled those worn by Smoky the Bear on the Forest Fire posters. The locals who were generally manning these traps were usually referred to as *"City Kitties"*. Most of the truckers bought radar detectors to go along with their CB radios and began using them in conjunction with the radio to keep them from getting speeding tickets.

The way it worked was one vehicle, truck or car, would take the lead and a convoy would be formed. Convoys could be as many as five or six vehicles. That person in the front vehicle was referred to as the *"Front door"*. That person would broadcast to the oncoming traffic a question. The dialog would usually go like this, "Breaker, breaker, Big John northbound on o'l 41 lookin' for a south bounder."

"Daddy Rabbit comin' back at ya'. What you see over yur shoulder Big John?"

By now, each person on the radio would recognize the other's voice.

Big John would answer, "Clean and green back to mile marker two-fifteen, how it be on your donky? Come back."

Daddy Rabbit would come back with an answer, "City Kitty around mile marker two-ninety-six."

Then there might be a little talk about the traffic congestion or even the weather, but in most cases, it would end with,

"Keep the shiny side up and the rubber side down, Big John on the side."

"Faster than a speeding turtle, stronger smelling than a musk ox, able to leap tire treads in a single bounce, Daddy Rabbit be gone."

Naturally, the whole convoy would hear this exchange and maybe one person in the convoy would comment.

The salesmen who were on the road at the same time as the truckers, soon found out that if they had a CB radio, they could listen in on the truckers and run with them at whatever speed they were going. It didn't take long for the truckers and the salesmen to begin co-operating together in their search for the Smokies. Many friendships were formed between the salesmen and the truckers when they would all meet at a truck-stop for coffee at the end of a long day on the road.

The CB radio worked moderately well, but there developed an unspoken rivalry between the Smokies and the *CB-ers*. Once the "Double Nickel" was abolished, the CB culture gradually went away

Stories Told by Traveling Salesmen

as the speed limit was raised, depending on the state, to 65 or 70 miles per hour.When I was traveling in the 1970's, I traveled seven states. At that time, I was in frequent contact with a lot of truckers and salesmen. I kept a log of the "Handles" of many of my CB friends. The following in alphabetical order are a few of them.

A: *Angle Iron, Easily, SC.*

B: *Barracuda, SC; Beaver Mechanic; Beech Nut, Macon, G.A.; Bere'rer Rabbit; Big Orange, Orangeburg, SC.; Bionic Water Melon; Black Bart; Blackhawk, OH; Blue Grass Kid, Knoxville, TN; Blue Marvel, Dalton, GA; blue Moose; Bo Jangles; Bo Peep; Brown Sugar, Atlanta; Bugs Bunny; Bull Whip, WI.*

C: *Candy Man, Willis, Canada; California Clipper, Snellville, GA; Camel Jockey, Cameroon, TX; Carolina Creeper, SC; Carolina Rebel; Carolina Mule Skinner; Cat Fish, Augusta, GA; Chattanooga Choo Choo Chattanooga, TN; Cherokee Rebel; Cherokee Warrior, North GA; Chicken Licken, N. Augusta, SC; Carolina Creeper, SC; Carolina Rebel; Connecting Rod; Country Boy Abbeville, SC; Country Bumpkin; Cookie Monster; Corn Bread, Bristol, TN; Casanova; Curley Top, Tifton, TN.*

D: *Daddy Rabbit; Double "B" Insurance Macon, GA; Double Bogie; Droopy Drawers.*

E: *Easy Money; Eight Ball; El Bolo, Mt. Pleasant, SC.*

F: *Fla. Blue Boy; Fla. Connection; Fla. Firecracker; Flagship; Fox Fire; Fox Hunter; Freedom Rider; Free Spirit.*

G: *GA Boy; GA Crackerjack Sales, Winder, GA; GA Robin, Tullahoma, TN; GA Runner; GA Wetback, Steel Sales, Decatur, GA; Gabby; Gladiator; Golden Eagle, Jenningsport, TN; Goldie Locks; Green Dragon, McCormick, SC; Green Hornet, Morristown, TN; Gypsy Junkie, Junk Dealer, Charleston, SC.*

Alan M. Oberdeck

H: Hangman SC; Hatchet, NY; Head Chess, GA; Harry Houdini.

K: Kodiak, GA.

L: Lady Road Runner; Left Wheel; Little John, Richmond, VA; Lone Wolf; Long John.

M: Magic Dragon, Chattanooga, TN; Mallard; Midnight Cowboy, Laurenburg, NC; Mr. Chips, Michigan; Mr. Whiskers.

N: Nail Bender; Night Crawler, Salesman; Night Stalker; No Handle, Springfield, IL.

O: Old Crow; Old Peddler, Ind. Chem. Jakes Isl. SC; One Chinaman; Orange Crusher; Oysterman, Hickory, NC.

P: Party Doll; Plough Boy, NC; Poison Ivey; Pop Top, Cleveland, TN.

R: Rainbow Ryder; Rambling Man, West TN; Rambling Wreck; Ranger 350; Red Dog, Raleigh, NC; Red Pepper; Red Ryder, Dalton, GA; Ringold One; Rubber Bumper, FL; Rubber Ducky; Running Eagle.

S: Scrap Iron Man, Furniture Salesman, Fulton County, GA; Sea Fox Wilmington, SC; Sewage Man; Share Cropper, Salesman, Lawrenceville, GA; Shoe Fly; Smoker Road Runner; Snow White, Nurse, Snellville GA; Snuffy Smith, Gainesville, GA; Soldier Boy, FL; Stinger, NC; Straight Shooter, Chattanooga, TN; Sugar Bear; Suit Case; Sun Dance; Super Spy; Swamp Rabbit, Decatur, GA.

T: T C Longhorn; Tennessee Auctioneer; Tennessee Transplant; Tennessee Toddy; TEXAS Dandy; Tiger, GA; The Hunter; Tom Cat; Turkey.

U: Underground Farmer

W: *Waco Man*; *West Texas Manager*; *Wheel Jockey*; *White Lemon*; *Wild Mule, Doraville, GA*; *Windjammer, Dalton, GA*; *Witchdoctor*; *Wood Chopper, TN*.

Y: *Yellow Bird*; *Yellow Jake*.

At that time, I was a salesman selling industrial diamonds. My handle was Ace of Diamonds. My call sign was KTZ 7509. I usually spent five days a week on the road, but I was usually home on weekends.

Breaker, Breaker

"Breaker ten, how's it looken' o'er your shoulder east bound? O'er."

"Put yur pedal to the medal – yur clean and green back to the 157 split! Daddy Rabbit said that. O'er."

"Daddy Rabbit she be looken' gud yur way. The last thing we saw was a City Kitty on the side in Town Creek. Lonesome Sam o'er an out."

I had my CB radio on and I was heading east with my *pedal-to-the-metal* driving from Florence, Alabama back to Atlanta. The cellphone and other modern ways of communicating had yet to be invented. The CB radio, short for Citizens Band radio was authorized in 1945 as a way that ordinary people could talk to each other without a telephone line. This was used by truckers and other people who regularly traveled to talk to persons up to 3 to 5 miles away.

The greatest part of the fuel crunch had come and gone, but in its wake was the 55 miles per hour national speed limit. Now, I don't want anyone to get the idea that we salesman drove around breaking the speed law with abandon in those days, but I believe it is safe to say that with our CB radios and Super Snooper radar detectors we *irritated* the heck out of the 55 miles per hour speed limit.

Of course, as I made my way towards Decatur, Alabama, heading for home after work, going east on U.S. Alt Highway 72, I was intent on making the best time possible. And to do this meant that I had to be right up there with the fastest cars and trucks.

"Breaker ten this is Lonesome Sam just a booken' it for Decatur an I be needin' me front door. Anybuddy can help?"

"Hey there *gud* buddy,"

Now this was back before the term *'gud buddy'* got such a bad connotation.

"This is Ace of Diamonds east bound on ol' 72 pedal-to-the-metal. What be yur 20? O'er."

For those of you who have never listened in on CB radio, the trucker's jargon was the standard road language. I had just told Lonesome Sam that I was traveling his way and wanted to know his location, his 1020 abbreviated to just 20. "Ace of Diamonds, I be just enterin' Town Creek, what be yur 20? O'er." "I be just leaving Town Creek, must have a mile on yu. Bring her on through. I couldn't put an eyeball on that City Kitty. Ace of Diamonds. O'er."

There I was, *Front Door*! I am the first in line and first to be seen by any Smokey looking at the highway with his radar gun. Now I am taking my turn at *front door* and I begin to become very watchful of what is ahead on the road.

"Hey there Lonesome Sam, there be a four-wheeler on the side – he be clean. Ace of Diamonds. O'er."

"Things be looken' gud back here, keep on pedallen'. Lonesome Sam. Out."

"Breaker west bound, what yu see o'er yur donkey? This is Ace of Diamonds looken'. O'er."

This drive from Florence to Atlanta can be a long and boring one. During these early years, I was diving as many as 70,000 miles a year in one car. When I sit in a car that long, trying to maintain 55 miles per hour, driving alone from place to place, I tend to either get bored, lonely, or very drowsy.

I started from Florence after my last call at about 5:30 p.m. Central Standard Time. It was November, and by the time I had a good start down the road, I had already lost most of the light of day. Now, as the darkness settled in my forward visibility became less and less. I had to rely more and more on my CB and my radar detector to avoid the Smokey. "Breaker, breaker west bound, what do yu see o'er yur shoulder? Ace of Diamonds be looken. O'er."

Still no answer."Lonesome Sam, nobody's answering. Ace of Diamonds. O'er."

Lonesome Sam had begun to fade in the distance. I guessed my pedal was closer to the metal than his. I checked the clock (*slang for speedometer*) and noticed I was on the 75 mile per hour side of 55. Either I needed a fast response from a west bounder, or I would have to reign in my urge to get home a little earlier.

I was still a good five to six hours from home if I could keep my average speed at 55 miles per hour. That was almost imposable due to the number of cities and towns I would pass through between here and Atlanta. The best I could do would be to reach Atlanta and home by 11:30 to 12:30 Eastern Standard Time. I slowed down a bit.

"Breaker, Breaker for a west bound eighteen-wheeler, yu got an east bounder a looken'. O'er."

Silence."Lonesome Sam, nobody's answering, Ace of Diamonds. O'er."

Suddenly, I heard this faint feminine voice through the static of the CB Radio. I listened and the transmission seemed to be coming closer.

"Breaker, Breaker for the Ace of Diamonds."

The faint voice came garbled through the static.

"Breaker for the Ace of Diamonds."

The faint voice came through the static again.

"You got the Ace of Diamonds, sweet thing, come back."

"Where are you Ace of Diamonds?" Came the reply.

"Breaker for Lonesome Sam one time, Ace of Diamonds calling. O'er."

"Ace of Diamonds this is Lonesome Sam. What can I do fer yu? O'er."

"Did yu hear that sweet thing that just called me? Ace of Diamonds. O'er."

"Didn't hear any sweet thing. Yur breaking up. Lonesome Sam out."

"It's clear to here Lonesome Sam, bring 'er on up. Ace of Diamonds. O'er."

"I'm pedlin' as fast as I can –*static–static*. O'er."

"Breaker fer that one sweet thing. Ace of Diamonds calling. O'er."

"Yu got her, come back."

"What's yur handle? Ace of Diamonds. O'er."

"Flower Lady, come back."

"Flower Lady, Ace of Diamonds is pedlin' yur way, an we have Lonesome Sam watching our back door. Come back."

"Honey Bun, yu just peddle on up here, I'm a waiting. Flower Lady. O'er."

There is nothing quite so stimulating on a long lonely night's drive than the sugar sweet flirtatious voice of a woman coming through the constant snapping, crackling, and hissing of the static on the speaker of your CB radio.

Now Lonesome Sam, bless his heart, was company and just listening and responding to him was keeping me marginally awake. Now, this voice, female, with an invitation, got the blood flowing.

"Flower Lady, Ace of Diamonds here, I'm pedlin' yur way fast as I can. How's it a looken'? O'er."

"Put the pedal to the metal, it's clean and green all the way. Flower Lady. O'er."

"Hey there sweet thing!" Came a gruff unfamiliar voice from the CB radio speaker. "Which way yu be a goin'? Come back."

It never fails, a sweet thing will bring all the termites out of the woodwork.

"I be going east bound on this ol' 72. Which way yu be headin'? Flower Lady. O'er."

"I be about to turn this here eighteen-wheeler around an follow yu wherever yu be goin! Casanova said that. O'er."

Women on the CB are not the only ones who like to flirt. Men also have a tendency to be very good at it also. "Appreciate the kind words Casanova. How it be looken' o'er yur shoulder? Flower Lady. O'er."

"Yu be clean an green back to Decatur. Decatur is where I got on – can't help yu any further. Yu sure yu don't want to do a flip and follow me to Memphis Flower Lady? Casanova out."

Screech, squawk, screech, screech, garble, garble screech. This happens a lot when too many people open their microphones and try to respond at the same time.

"Breaker, Breaker for the one Casanova, Lonesome Sam callin'."

"Hey there Lonesome Sam, yu'r late getting to the junkyard – the dispatcher told me to have yu give him a land line as soon as I come across yur ugly face tonight Casanova. O'er."

"Yu just watch how yu talk to me or I'll tell the missus how yu been a sweet-talking Flower Lady. Lonesome Sam. O'er."

"How's it a looken' o'er yur donkey, Lonesome Sam? Casanova. O'er."

I was riding along listening to this talk, pedal to the metal, just dying to get back to Flower Lady, but I just don't break in on truckers when they are talking about road conditions, i.e. Smokies.

"She be clean an green back to Florence, Casanova. Yu keep the shiny side up an the rubber side down, Lonesome Sam. Down an out."

"Lonesome Sam, yu keep it tween the ditches ya' hear! Casanova down an on the side."

"Breaker, breaker for Flower Lady. Ace of Diamonds calling."

"You got her, come back. O'er."

"What yu be drivin'? Ace of Diamonds. O'er."

"A tan four-wheeler. Flower Lady. O'er."

"Flower Lady, look in yur rear view mirror an watch the lights. Ace of Diamonds. O'er."

"That's a big 10-4. Be a gentleman an peddle up here to take my front door. Flower Lady. O'er."

At that request from that honey sweet voice coming through the air, I just had to be a gentleman and pass her to take the front door position. This request was really easy as this section of 72 was four lane divided highway. Also, I was curious to see what was in that four-wheeler that looked so funny through the back window.

I guess like most salesmen I know, I always look over to my right and check out the driver of the car I am passing. I don't know why I do that, but I guess it is just one of those weird things some of us do. In any case, as I passed the beige four-wheeler being driven by Flower Lady, I looked to see what she had in her back seat. In the failing light of the evening, it looked like a jungle back there.

As I passed, I also tried to size up Flower Lady sitting behind the wheel in the front seat. In the darkness, I couldn't make out much about her. She looked to be rather young. Her hair was short and appeared to be neatly styled. She wore glasses with fancy frames. I couldn't tell what color her hair was, but I could eliminate blond and gray.

She sat low in the seat which would indicate she was probably shorter than average. This was reinforced by the fact that her seat was positioned rather close to the steering wheel. Her left hand was in the 11:00 position on the steering wheel which allowed me to judge that she might not be married as her ring finger seemed to be bare. Her right hand was still holding the microphone in a position which would make it ready to use at a moment's notice. Usually, when I look at a woman in a car I pass, I can even get an idea of her build, however, she sat so low in the seat and the light was so bad, I couldn't even guess.

I figured she was probably a very outgoing young lady. Just because she came on strong on the CB, didn't mean anything. Shy people tend to lose their inhibitions when talking on the CB, so you can't tell. What I saw that gave me the impression that she was outgoing, was the type of jewelry she was wearing. Her earrings hung down to her shoulders and were very reflective in the little light available. She had flashy diamond-type rings on several of her fingers. She just wasn't adorned like a shy wallflower.

To be honest, I didn't pass her to be a gentleman and take her front door, I passed her because I wanted to get home to my wife at a reasonable hour and she was peddling much too slow to be my front door.

"Flower Lady, Ace of Diamonds here. I just took yur doors. O'er."

"Ace of Diamonds, does that little car go that fast or is my clock wrong? Flower Lady. O'er."

"Yes an no in that order, Ace of Diamonds. O'er."

"Ace of Diamonds, does that antenna ever scrape the bottom of the clouds an cause rain? Flower Lady asking. O'er."

"Yu like my whip? Ace of Diamonds. O'er."

"Ace of Diamonds, yu couldn't have found a longer antenna or a smaller four-wheeler to put it on, could yu? Flower Lady. O'er."

"I keep looken', but this is the best I can find. Yu got Tarzan asleep in that jungle in the back of yur four-wheeler? O'er."

By that comment, I was just checking to see if she had any male passengers along for the ride.

"Breaker, breaker ten fer an east bounder on this ol' 72, yu got Shade Tree a looken'. O'er."

"Yu got Ace of Diamonds east bound, come back."

"How's it looken' o'er yur donkey? O'er."

"There was a report of some activity of the City Kitty in Town Creek, but I didn't put an eyeball on it. Yu be clean an green back to Florence. How's it be looken' on yur back door gud buddy? Ace of Diamonds. O'er."

Shade Tree, that was his handle. There are times when you hear a handle once and when you go to respond, you can't remember it on the spur of the moment so you respond with good buddy.

"Put the pedal to the metal, she be clean an green back to Decatur. Shade Tree. O'er."

"We thank yu for them kind words, Shade Tree. Yu have yurself a good night an keep the shiny side up an the rubber side down. Ace of Diamonds. O'er."

"Breaker fer Flower Lady, Ace of Diamonds callin'."

"Yu got her, come back. O'er."

"Yu get all them gud words, come back."

"10-4 Ace of Diamonds, Flower Lady. O'er."

"Breaker fer Flower Lady, this is Shade Tree callin'."

"Yu got her, come back."

"Yu out a Music City? Come back."

"That's a negative, I was out of Florence, but I am moving. Flower Lady out."

"Just a checkin'. I used to talk to a Flower Lady from Music City all the time, but I haven't heard from her in months an I thought yu might be her. Shade Tree. O'er."

"I used to just stay around Florence. Flower Lady. O'er."

"What yu be drivin' Flower Lady? O'er."

"I'm in a tan Chevy four-wheeler. Flower Lady. O'er."

"Flower Lady, yu just pull right up behind me an I'll buy yu coffee at the next truck stop. Shade Tree. O'er."

"I'm east bound runnin' with the Ace of Diamonds. Flower Lady. O'er."

"Just my luck, all the sweet things are runnin' away from me tonight, Shade Tree. O'er."

"Don't feel bad now. How bout I take a rain check on that Shade Tree? Flower Lady. O'er."

"Sounds gud to me. Flower Lady yur startin' to break up, so have a safe one. Shade Tree over and on the side."

I was still driving along, watching my radar detector. Looking at the road in front, watching for moving traffic, and looking in the mirror at the lights of Flower Lady in my rear. I was growing fond of her voice and really don't want to lose her.

"How far yu be a headin' Flower Lady? Ace of Diamonds askin'."

"I be headin' for big A town. Flower Lady. O'er."

'How yu plannin' on goin'? Ace of Diamonds. O'er."

"To Huntsville and then Rome. O'er."

"I be a headin' to big A town myself. Ace of Diamonds. O'er."

"I'll be bringin' up yur back door. Flower Lady said that. O'er."

"This be Ace of Diamonds KTZ 7509 on the air."

According to the Citizens Band law, all people owning a CB radio were licensed by the Federal Government and occasionally were supposed to identify themselves. It had been a while since I had done that, so I made that announcement at that time.

"Breaker, breaker ten fer a west bounder on this ol' 72. Ace of Diamonds looken'."

I turned down the squelch to see if there were any responses out in the weeds, but all I heard from the speaker was more static. It was around 6:30 p.m. and most people were probably home eating supper by now. Besides, we were getting near the big city of Decatur, Alabama and the background clutter would make it necessary to adjust the squelch to the point that the static through the speaker was bearable which meant it was impossible to have more than a mile range on any broadcast.

"Breaker fer the flower Lady, Ace of Diamonds callin'."

"Yu got her! Come in. O'er."

"We be comin' up to Decatur. How far yu be goin' tonight? Ace of Diamonds. O'er."

"I be goin' till I get tired Ace. O'er."

"I be goin' through Decatur takin 31 North an then headin' for Huntsville. Yu be comin'? Ace of Diamonds. O'er."

Sometimes after talking to a woman for a while, the ego begins to work and a salesman or a trucker would begin to feel protective of the ladies out on the road. I had begun to get some of those feelings.

"I be following yu. Flower Lady. O'er."

The drive through Decatur got rather noisy, and the continuous chatter and banter on the CB did nothing but keep me silent as I proceeded through the town. I watched in the mirror and could see by the streetlights more of what flower lady was carrying in her car. It appeared to be full of flowers, ferns, or at least plants. Flower Lady did keep up with me through the traffic, though.

"Hey there Flower Lady, we finally made it out of the noise on the CB, so I figured I'd lay some words on yu. Ace of Diamonds. O'er."

"Thought I'd lost yu at that one light, but yu were hidden in front of that ten-wheeler. Flower Lady. O'er."

"Breaker, breaker ten one time fer a west bounder on ol' Alt. 72, yu got an east bounder a looken'. O'er."

I stayed off the microphone for a time to wait for a response and none came.

"Breaker, breaker ten fer a west bound eighteen-wheeler on ol' Alt. 72, yu got an East bound four-wheeler a looken'. Ace of Diamonds. O'er."

"Breaker fer the Flower Lady. Ace of Diamonds callin'."

"Yu got me Ace. Flower Lady. O'er."

"Things are pretty quiet out here now; everyone must be home eating. I doubt that the Smokies are home though. I'm going to back it down closer to the double nickel for a while. Ace of Diamonds. O'er."

I have always tried to be a careful driver so as not to accumulate any more speeding tickets than necessary, so I reigned the speed back and adjusted the sensitivity on the radar detector.

The sweet as honey sounding voice came out of the speaker again,

"Ace of Diamonds, yu getting hungry? Flower Lady. O'er."

"Sure thing, Flower Lady. Ace of Diamonds. O'er."

"How bout we stop in Huntsville an get a bite to eat? Flower Lady. O'er."

Again, this was said with a sultry sounding voice.

"Okay by me. Ace of Diamonds. O'er."

I wasn't in the mood for a sit-down meal which would cost me precious time. I desired to get home as soon as I could, but many things are said on the CB that are never acted on. At this point, I wondered a little more about what that Flower Lady had in mind. I checked the setting on my radar detector one more time and increased my speed a little.

"Flower Lady, what yu be doin' with all that foliage in yur four-wheeler? Ace of Diamonds. O'er."

"I be moving to Gainesville Georgia an the movers couldn't pack these plants. Flower Lady. O'er."

"Where be yur better half? Ace of Diamonds. O'er."

"He be left in Florence with his girlfriend an divorce papers. Honey, I be free! Flower Lady. O'er."

Now, that was not the response I expected, but this increased my curiosity and heightened my interest in hearing her story. It should keep me awake for quite a while.

"Breaker, breaker fer channel ten yu got an east bound looken' on Alt. 72 for a front door. Ace of Diamonds lookeen'. O'er."

"Yu got (*squawk squeak garble*) out."

"Ace of Diamonds to that come back, yu broke up. O'er."

"Yu got Harry (*garble, garble*) on yur front (*garble*)"

I increased my speed a little and waited a couple of minutes to try again and race this person ahead of me.

"Breaker fer that one Harry, Ace of Diamonds calling. O'er."

"Yu got one Harry Houdini headin' fer Huntsville. O'er."

"Yu got Ace of Diamonds and Flower Lady on yur donkey. It's looking good back here. O'er."

"Yu clean and green to here, bring it on up. Harry Houdini said that. O'er."

"Did yu hear that Flower Lady? Ace of Diamonds. O'er."

"It was garbled. Flower Lady. O'er."

"Harry Houdini what's yur 20? Ace of Diamonds. O'er."

"Ace of Diamonds yu are getting clearer, yu must be a couple a miles behind and gaining on me. What yu in? Harry Houdini. O'er."

"I be in a four-wheeler. What yu be drivin? Ace of Diamonds. O'er."

"I be a four-wheeler. Harry Houdini. O'er."

"How's the front door a looken'? Ace of Diamonds. O'er."

"Breaker fer a west bounder on this Alt. 72, Harry Houdini be looken'. O'er"

I waited for a comeback or even a garbled noise of someone ahead of Harry Houdini trying to come back, but nothing. I decided to pedal a little faster and at least put an eyeball on Harry Houdini.

"Harry Houdini, I'm a comin' yur way. Ace of Diamonds. O'er."

"Ace of Diamonds your breaking up. Flower Lady. O'er."

"Flower Lady put the pedal to the metal, yur clean an green to here. Ace of Diamonds. O'er."

"Harry Houdini, we have Flower Lady on the back door. Ace of Diamonds. O'er."

"Ace of Diamonds bring it on up. Flower Lady, keep on truckin'. Harry Houdini. O'er."

"Harry Houdini, look in the mirror and I'll blink. Ace of Diamonds. O'er."

"Ace of Diamonds, I got an eyeball on yu. Harry Houdini. O'er."

"Harry Houdini, how far yu be goin'? Ace of Diamonds. O'er."

"I be headin' home to Scottsboro. How far yu be goin'? Harry Houdini. O'er."

"I be headin' to the big A town. Ace of Diamonds. O'er."

"Breaker fer the Harry Houdini, Flower Lady callin'. O'er."

"Yu got him sweet thing. Harry Houdini. O'er."

"Yu from Scottsboro? Flower Lady. O'er."

"I was from Muscle Shoals, but I moved to Scottsboro a while back. It is more the center of my territory. Harry Houdini. O'er."

"I'm movin' from Florence to Gainesville, Georgia. I used to talk to you in Florence. I used to go by Sweet Sue. Flower Lady. O'er."

"I thought you sounded familiar. So, the old man is movin' to Gainesville? I didn't think anything could blast him out of Florence. Harry Houdini. O'er."

"The old man is staying in Florence with his girlfriend and his divorce papers, and I'm going to Gainesville. Flower Lady. O'er."

I'm following Harry Houdini and he wasn't making very good time. The double nickel just wasn't making it for me. I decided to tune in my radar detector finer and take the front door.

"Harry Houdini, I'm gonna take yur front door. Ace of Diamonds. O'er."

With that statement I passed his big white four-wheeler and set a faster pace.

"Flower Lady, how did yu become Flower Lady? Harry Houdini. O'er."

"I packed my stuff in a moving van, but I had to load all my plants into my four-wheeler and I just decided to call myself Flower Lady. O'er."

"Breaker for a west bound, Ace of Diamonds looken'. O'er."

"Yu be clean and green back to the Space Center. How it looken' o'er yur donkey? The Flash be askin'. O'er."

"Thank yu fer those gud words Flash, she be clean and green back to Decatur, Ace of Diamonds. O'er."

"Breaker fer the one Flower Lady. Did yu get that last comeback? Ace of Diamonds. O'er."

"Came through loud an clear, Flower Lady. O'er."

"Flower Lady, how come yur movin' to Gainesville? Harry Houdini be askin'. O'er."

"Got a gud job offer an couldn't turn it down. Anyway, this puts me far away from the ex. It was final today, an I am free an want to kick up my heels tonight! Flower Lady. O'er."

"Breaker ten fer a west bounder. Ace of Diamonds be looken'. O'er."

"Breaker breaker fer a west bounder. Ace of Diamonds be callin'. O'er."

Things were dead at this time of the evening. It seemed as if we were the only travelers on the CB.

"Ace of Diamonds, how long before we get to Huntsville, this Flower Lady be getting' pretty famished? O'er."

"Probably bout thirty minutes, what do you think Harry? Ace of Diamonds. O'er."

"That be bout right, Harry Houdini. O'er."

"Breaker fer Harry Houdini, do you know a good place to stop an eat? I feel like havin' a party! Flower Lady. O'er."

"There's one right downtown. It should be servin' until bout 9:00 tonight. Been there, the steaks are gud. Harry Houdini. O'er."

"Sound gud to yu Ace? Flower Lady. O'er."

"I'd like to help yu kick up yur heels, but I am runnin' late an will have to pass on that. Ace of Diamonds. O'er."

"Just put yur eyeballs on my donkey an I'll get yu there. Harry Houdini. O'er."

I increased my speed a little.

"Where yu stayin' in Scottsboro? (*garble, squeak*) Flo... (*squeak garble*). O'er."

I had had the pedal to the metal and was fast leaving them behind. I needed to make up some time and if they couldn't keep up that was too bad. Maybe they will have a nice dinner in Huntsville, and who knows what that could lead to.

As I approached Huntsville the static on the CB increased, and the extraneous radar signals excited my radar detector to the point that I decided to slow down a bit and change the sensitivity.

I had just passed through Huntsville when I decided to stop at a Quick Stop for some motion lotion (gas for the car), a donut, and a coke. I checked the CB for noise, reset the squelch on the CB, and reset the sensitivity on my radar detector.

"Breaker, breaker ten fer a west bound on 72, yu got an east bound a looken'. Ace of Diamonds. O'er."

"Breaker, breaker fer a west bounder on 72, Ace of Diamonds be looken'. O'er."

"Ace of Diamonds yu got Spaceman out of Huntsville travelin' west. How's it looken' o'er yur donkey? Spaceman. O'er."

"Yu be clean an green back to Huntsville. How's it looken' o'er yur donkey? Ace of Diamonds. O'er."

"I put an eyeball on some action with the City Kitty outside a Woodville, that's all I be seeing. Spaceman, O'er."

"Thank yu fer the kind words Spaceman. Keep the shiny side up and the rubber side down. Ace of Diamonds. O'er."

"Same ta yu. Spaceman said that! I be faster than a speedin' turtle, able to jump large tire treads with a single bounce, stronger smellin' than a Musk Ox, and prone to pass water at the sight of a Smoky! I be gone."

"Breaker, breaker ten, Ace of Diamonds east bound looken' fer a front door, come back. O'er."

It was getting late and the traffic on the road was light. I didn't see anything at Woodville, and I didn't get any response to any of my calls. The CB was quiet all the way to Scottsboro.

After Scottsboro I began to become tired and continued to try to raise someone on the CB, but to no avail. The highway I was on was not a well traveled trucker's route, so I didn't hear anything until Fort Payne.

"Breaker, breaker ten, yu got the Ace of Diamonds east bound on 35 lookin', come back. O'er."

"Yu got the Spring Chicken, come back. O'er."

Came a soft sultry voice through my speaker.

"Hey there Spring Chicken, which way yu goin' on this ol' 35? Ace of Diamonds. O'er."

That comeback awakened me and probably got a little needed adrenaline flowing in my blood stream.

"I'm stuck right here, Ace. Stop by and have a coffee at the truck stop on 11. We have the best coffee in Fort Payne don't yu know. Spring Chicken. O'er."

"I'd like to take yu up on that, but I'm headin' fer A town and I can't spare the time. Ace of Diamonds. O'er."

"That's too bad, Ace. We could sure spice up yur trip if yu stop by! Spring Chicken. O'er."

"How it be looken' back to Rome, have yu heard anything? Ace of Diamonds. O'er."

"Traffic's been light, haven't heard a thing. Maybe if yu stop by, that might change. Spring Chicken. O'er."

It sounded to me that Spring Chicken might be selling more than just coffee as she was using a syrupy sounding voice, trying to lure me in for that coffee. Very soon, I was out of range.

I took highway 35 to highway 9 which turned into Georgia 20 at the state line to Rome. Then I took 20/411 to Cartersville where I picked up Highway 41 into Atlanta. After Rome, the voice traffic on the CB became so much that I couldn't broadcast for more than a mile. It didn't matter as the traffic was moving way faster than the double nickel and that was fine with me. I turned the squelch up so I could only hear the conversation that was close. I turned on the AM radio and tuned it to WSB to look for any traffic problems that might be broadcast for my drive through Atlanta. As I left Atlanta I again got on the CB, but nobody answered my calls. When I reached home at about 12:30 a.m., I got on the CB one more time. I followed the spirit of the law and announced, "This is KTZ 7509. Down and out."

The Day of Change

Late Sunday night, I finally closed my home office and finished packing my briefcase for Monday's trip and set it on a chair. The clothing to be worn in the morning was laid out on top of it. The wife and kids were already in bed and asleep. I then set my alarm for 4:30 a.m. and joined my wife in bed. I was tired, but sleep would not come easy. I tossed and turned.

"*I'll make up for lack of sleep on the plane,*" I told myself.

The alarm awakened me at 4:30 a.m. and I reacted to it as fast as I can so I won't awaken my wife. As it was, she grunted, rolled over, wished me a good trip, kissed me goodbye, and went right back to sleep. I dressed as quietly as I could, grabbed my suite case, and headed down the hall to my office. There, I picked up my briefcase and, in the darkness, stumbled my way out of the house to my car.

I was programmed, suitcase and briefcase in the trunk, driver in the front seat, and car in motion to the Post Office. At the Post Office, I mailed the letters I had written over the weekend and pick up any Saturday mail from the company's P. O. Box. The forty-minute drive to the airport Park-n-Fly was routine. The ride to Atlanta Hartsfield Airport on the Park-n-Fly shuttle worked like a charm. And by 8:30 a.m., I was comfortable in my seat in a Delta Airlines plane and on my way to St. Louis, Missouri. As soon as the plane left the ground, I was asleep.

The week of September 9, 2001 was the type of week I really enjoyed. The company I worked for had a contract to supply Compressed Air Treatment products to a major Air Compressor Manufacturer headquartered in the Mississippi Rivertown of Quincy, Illinois.

This company was holding a product training week for its distributor's sales force. There would be salespeople from all over the U.S. attending. As a part of that meeting, they had planned a product training school for the Compressed Air Treatment Products that they private labeled from us. I was the teacher, their school began Monday morning. My part of the schooling was to begin on Tuesday and continue until Thursday noon.

The plan was for me to fly into St. Louis on Monday and in a Hertz Rental Car, drive to Quincy. I would spend Tuesday morning training the inside salespeople on the product line and begin to train the Distributor Salesmen in the afternoon. Thursday, I would leave Quincy at noon and drive back to St. Louis and fly home on a Delta flight that evening. The reason I really enjoyed those sales training weeks was because I could interact and get feedback from so many people in such a short time.

The plane landed in St. Louis on time. I picked up my luggage and was on my way in the Hertz rental car a little after noon. I stopped for a quick lunch and was checked in at my hotel in Quincy on time, and called over to the plant to double-check the next day's schedule. Naturally, there was a change in the schedule. They asked that I come to the office at 9:00 a.m. and not at 8:00 as planned, as there were some things needed to be done before I was to begin my training.

Quincy, Illinois is on Central Daylight Savings time, so I set my alarm clock accordingly. Everything was in place and this trip was going so smoothly that it was turning out to be one of the best one I had recently. I went to sleep confident that everything was going to work well.

I awakened before the alarm went off. And followed my morning hotel routine, grabbed my briefcase, and went down to breakfast in the hotel dining room. I ate my usual breakfast, and as I was early, this gave me time to read a part of the USA Today newspaper. At about 8:30, I got into my rental car and drove to the plant.

I parked in the Visitor's lot and climbed the stairs to the third-floor location of the Marketing Department where I would train the inside sales staff for half a day. I entered the large room filled with desks where the inside salespeople worked the phones. I expected to see them each working at their desks doing what inside salespeople do. Instead, I entered a room filled with a confused buzz.

"Did you hear anything on the radio on your way in?" someone asked me.

"It's a rental car and I didn't try to find a news station this morning. It was such a short drive, so I just left it off." I answered.

"I just got the TV station on the TV in the conference room!" someone excitedly announced."What is all the confusion about?" I asked a person arranging his papers at a phone desk.

"A minute ago, Bill's wife called the office and told him to turn on a radio or something because NBC News just reported that an airplane has hit one of the towers of The World Trade Center in New York, City." he excitedly exclaimed.

"Oh, that is probably a small plane accident. You know, a twin-engine airplane flew into the side of The Empire State Building in a fog during World War II. There was no permanent damage." I naively answered, thinking nothing of the information.

Before I could make any more stupid statements, someone announced he had the small TV in the conference room working. Everyone who could, headed there. When I got to the conference room, the small group had gathered in front of the small TV. They were watching in disbelief at the pictures on the TV screen. And I couldn't believe my eyes either, as I saw the smoke and flames coming from the tower. I believe we were all in shock.

Then, a little after 9:00 a. m. Central Daylight Time, as we were standing around the TV watching the first tower burn, the second plane hit the south tower. We all stood there in horror as we watched this happen. The next airplane seemed to have flown directly into the second tower as though it was flown there on purpose.

Sometime after 9:00, it was decided that if any work was to get done, one of the men would work in the conference room near the TV. If something else happens, it would be his job to let us all know. Still in a state of shock, we all went back to work.

I worked with part of the inside sales staff reviewing with them the right procedures to obtain the correct information to complete an order for our product. I would work with this part of the staff for an hour while the others handled the phones and then they would switch. We were settling down and beginning to concentrate on what we were supposed to be doing.

We were still in a state of shock, but things were getting done. Then the fellow stationed in the conference room excitedly announced that another plane just flew into the Pentagon. That announcement took us back to the TV for a long look, more chaos, and more confusion followed. It seemed like no one was answering the phones. It was decided that it was necessary for all of us to get back to work. Again, one person would be working with the TV news in the background.

Then it was announced that all air traffic had been grounded. The planes in flight were instructed to land at the nearest airport. At first, the on-air commentators had no idea of what to tell the people watching so there was a lot of speculation as to whether this was a foreign attack or something else.

The management of the company wisely decided that:

1. Quincy, IL was not directly affected.
2. There was no way any of us were going to fly anywhere.
3. As long as I was there to do the training, we should concentrate on that.
4. We should wait to see what was happening before changing anything with the Sales Training schedule for the next two days.

More and more disturbing reports were coming in from the newscasts. All commercial flights were grounded until this was investigated. No, all commercial flights were grounded until Wednesday afternoon. No, that proved false, no one knew when the commercial flights would resume. Where was President Bush? He was criticized for not going to Washington, etc. He was criticized for not acting soon enough. He was criticized, criticized and criticized!

Noon arrived and I ate lunch in the company cafeteria with the inside sales staff. We were still in mild shock over what we had just experienced. It was all we could talk about. After a short lunch, I went across the street to the training building to meet the distributor salesmen that I was to train. They were standing around in groups waiting for me to arrive. Their conversation centered around the latest news.

As many of them had flown into Quincy from various cities around the country, their first big concern was how they were going to get home; I expressed the same concern. No one had any answers. There were no radios or broadcast TV's in the training room. We would have to wait until the class ended to find out anything more.

We covered the material that was planned for that afternoon and continued to follow the scheduled material despite the confusion surrounding the planes and the outside world. At the end of the session, someone came over from the Marketing Department and gave us the latest news. It was so confusing that it was no help at all.

As was the custom, the company took those attending the training to a nice restaurant on the Mississippi Riverbank for what was to be a great evening meal. Usually, these dinners were the time when the attendees would discuss among themselves aspects of what they had learned in the training sessions. This night the buzz could be summed up as *"How am I going to get home?"* The subject of *"When will I get home?"* hadn't even come up yet. The cloud of uncertainty hung like a dense fog over dinner.

Because of the time difference and the length of time spent eating we missed the televised Presidential address given by President Bush.

All I heard from the news on TV was that this seemed to be an attack on the U.S. government by some terrorists. And no one was jumping into any conclusions. The second piece of information was that no domestic flights would be taking place any time soon.

I called home to talk to my wife and listen as she described the latest happenings at home. We talked about what I had heard from the television news in my room and she passed on the rumors she had heard from the news she was watching. We discussed the horror of the attack on the Twin Towers, the Pentagon, and the plane that had crashed in the field in Pennsylvania. We about talked what the attack meant for us and how it would affect us. It was not a short call.

Finally, the last question she asked was the one that had been on my mind all day, *how would I get home on Thursday*? I had a ticket on the Delta flight from St. Louis, but if no commercial flights were allowed, of what use was it? I told her I would see if I could arrange something with Hertz tomorrow so I would have a car to drive to Atlanta on Thursday. We left it at that, and I hung up the phone.

Wednesday morning, I listened to the TV in my hotel room, but could find out nothing as to when commercial air travel would begin. There was talk of some flights happening during the afternoon, but this all seemed to be speculations. When the decision had been made to ground all commercial air traffic, airplanes were ordered to land at the next available airport. This resulted in many large airplanes having landed at airports scattered all over the country.

Many of these airports had no facilities to service them. Unscrambling this mess was almost like trying to sort boiled spaghetti noodles into straight lines again. The planes needed to be ferried back to their home bases, inspected, and serviced before they could be inserted back into the airline schedules.

At around 7:00 a.m., I got on the phone with Hertz in St. Louis. I discussed the situation with the agent, and we changed my reservations. The old reservation had me turning in the rental car I had in St. Louis and going to the airport to catch my flight home. What I had was a small St. Louis based car that Hertz didn't want driven to Atlanta.

We agreed that I would turn that car in at St. Louis and replace it with a car that was to be relocated to Atlanta. I was guaranteed this car and was given a Hertz contract number. By the time I arrived at the training room, I was confident that if I drove all night Thursday, I would arrive in Atlanta sometime Friday morning.

This was not the case with the majority of the Distributor Salesmen I was instructing. They had no idea when they would arrive home. The morning session was interrupted several times when my students tried to make travel arrangements for Thursday. For them, it was finding out from their companies what kind of arrangements could be made to get them home and at what cost.

Most of them had flown into the small Quincy airport on Sunday. They were then picked up by the hotel shuttle. They had no rental car that they could leverage or extend to get them out of Quincy. When they checked, there were no rental cars available either. It seemed some of them would not get home for days. By the end of class on Wednesday, Thursday travel was still up in the air for most of them.

The classes were kept pretty much to the scheduled subjects, but the breaks were a time of sharing of the latest info. This came if someone had information from a cell phone call or if someone in another part of the building reported something he had just heard on the radio. That evening, we ate as a group again.

At these dinners, we would discuss some of the things learned that day, but this night all that was on everyone's mind was the terror attack, the horror of the deaths of the passengers in the ill-fated planes, the plight of the people who worked in the two towers, the people that took down the plane in Pennsylvania, and the people in the Pentagon building.

After we broke up, I went to my room, called my wife, and watched what I could on TV. At this point, it was as though I was mesmerized by what I was seeing. The newsmen seemed to keep repeating themselves divulging nothing new and yet I couldn't tear myself away from watching. I awakened around 3:00 a.m., I was still half-sitting with the pillows propped behind me on the bed.

I had fallen asleep there, watching the continuous reporting on the news. I turned the TV off and nestled into the covers to go back to sleep. I got up early, spruced myself up for the day, packed my suitcase for the trip home, went to the dining room, and ate breakfast. I arrived at the training room early. At least I was confident that I could make it home on Friday. The travel plans for most of the others were still yet to be solved.

We began the class on time and everyone there appeared to have had a long night; probably having sat up in bed watching the news as I had. We covered the material rather fast as it seemed no one had a lot of questions and everyone wanted to try to find ways to head home. About halfway through the session, I was pulled out of the classroom for an urgent message from my wife.

I immediately called her back to find out what kind of family emergency she was dealing with.

"She never interrupted me for anything so this must be something bad", I thought. The message she had for me was the one she received from Delta Airlines in Atlanta asking me to call a special phone number. I typed the number into my cell phone and listened as the number rang.

"Hello," the agent answered.

"Hello, my name is Alan M. Oberdeck. And I got a message to call this number," I answered.

"Wait a moment while I look you up. Aha! here you are. You were scheduled to fly to Atlanta this evening. Is that right?" the agent asked.

"That's right," I responded.

"Delta had an international flight that had to land at the closest airport which happened to be St. Louis when all the flights were grounded. That plane will be cleared to be ferried back to Atlanta this evening. You are a Gold Frequent Flyer and can have a seat on that airplane if you are not afraid to fly," he explained.

"I am not afraid to fly. What time do I need to be there?" I replied.

"The flight leaves at 7:00, can you be at the gate by 6:30?" the agent asked.

"I will be there," I replied.

"Very good, check in at the counter," the agent instructed.

"Thank you," I replied as I ended the call.

I then called Hertz St. Louis and talked to an agent explaining the situation, making the car I had reserved available for someone who had no other way to Atlanta.

Needless to say, this good news made the rest of the day much less stressful. I finished the class at noon as planned, caught a fast-food hamburger on the way to St. Louis, and turned in my rental car at the airport Hertz. Hertz was not running any shuttles to the airport, so an employee drove me to the airport in my rental car.

When I arrived, the airport was empty. It was like a morgue, spooky. Even when I came into an airport late at night there were always more people around. When I presented myself at the Delta counter to check in for my flight, I had to get the attention of someone. I found out that there was no protocol established yet, so the only people invited for this ride to Atlanta were the people Delta vouched for. There were seventeen of us, and our luggage was checked through. We could carry our briefcases and were boarded.

It was about 10:15 p.m. on September 13, 2001 when I arrived at baggage claim in Atlanta airport to retrieve my luggage from the carousel. Hartsfield Airport still had some activity, from where I don't know. I was approached by one of the Atlanta news stations and was asked if I was a frequent flyer. I indicated that I was.

Then I was asked about my reaction to what had taken place in the air during the past week. I remember talking to the camera for several minutes. I know that I got my fifteen seconds of fame as it is still recorded on tape somewhere in my collection of obsolete VCR tapes. For the life of me, I can't remember what I said on the snippet they broadcasted.

It was several months before my company allowed any of us in the field to fly again. The airline flights were resumed, but at that point I was covering my seventeen states by car. This meant I would leave on Sunday and get home on Saturday. When the flights were resumed, there were new rules for everyone to follow. This was the beginning of the hell we all must now go through to travel by air any place in the world. September 11, 2001 was the *"Day of Change"*.

The Trip to Memphis

It has been the practice for a group of retired salesmen to meet occasionally for coffee at a local coffee shop. We usually sit around a table and comment on the current happenings and remember how things were when we were still active. One of the fellows commented that he had to fly from Atlanta to Milwaukee to handle some legal situation and would be gone for several days.

We gave him our condolences for the fact that he was going to have to fly. Each of us had traveled a lot when we had been selling and commented on the sorry state of current airline travel. We wished him well and generally kidded around with him about flying.

One from our group, who had had a large territory, usually more than seventeen states, lamented on how difficult air travel has become and he told this story. Air travel used to be simple. It was fast, efficient, effective, and sometimes fun. Let me tell you about one of the trips I remember.

It was in the winter during the late 1970s and I had appointed a new distributor in my territory. This was a trip to meet and spend a day with the sales managers in the key cities where they operated. The trip entailed flying from Atlanta to Charleston, SC, to Richmond, VA, to Knoxville, TN, to Memphis, TN and then back to Atlanta. In each city, I would get a rental car and try to keep it only 24 hours so as not to incur extra rental charges.

The weather was good for the first two days, but a front had moved in, and my day in Knoxville was cold and blustery with the forecast of snow in the late afternoon. Fortunately, I was done with my meetings early and was able to head to the Knoxville airport before the snow flurries began. I turned my car in early, around 4:00 p. m., even though my flight didn't leave until around 8:00.

The old Knoxville airport had a lounge area that overlooked the gate area and was not restricted to only airline passengers as is now the case in all airports. I was able to go there to kill the time with some comfort before my flight.

Knoxville was not the busiest airport, but it had planes in and out all afternoon and evening. Therefore, there were many people coming in and out of the lounge as they waited to meet people coming in on the next flight, and those waiting to leave on the next flight. Being a sort of gregarious person, I was able to kill time talking to many people as they came and went.

It was around 6:30 that the people coming into the lounge began to be other salesmen who were also on the 8:00 flight. Being salesmen, we congregated in one area where we could talk about mutual concerns, tell jokes, have something to eat and drink, and watch out of the window for the arrival of the plane which would take each of us to our next city.

As the gray cloud cover was losing the illumination it was receiving as the sun began to set, the snow began to fall faster, and our little corner of the world seemed to become warmer and cozier as the evening wore on. In what light was left through the falling snow which had began to accumulate, the scene beyond the glass wall took on a peaceful air.

At the edge of where the airport flood lights shown, we could see a bedraggled looking airplane parked out of the way over at one corner of the airfield. It appeared as though this little airplane was being stored there. It was a twin-engine low wing airplane, an old Martin 404. From what we could see, it had two gasoline powered radial engines.

We could make out the name Southern Airlines in big letters on the side. Although I had flown a lot, I usually flew either on Eastern or Delta airlines and had very little experience with Southern Airlines. After all, most of the airlines at this time used jet airplanes and those with propellers such as the Convair 580 or 600, were powered by turbojet engines and were referred to as turboprop airplanes.

So, when I saw that bedraggled-looking Martin 404 airplane sitting over in the corner with its piston engines, I just assumed that it was being stored. Several of the other salesmen shared that opinion and we began making that plane the butt of our jokes and comments.

One of the fellows wondered if that type of plane was used for freight service. Another questioned was what the cost of storing something that old at the airport would be. Someone thought that that might be part of an air museum, and we all laughed. Another plane landed and people deplaned, the plane was then serviced, and about twenty minutes later, was boarded and left for another destination.

It was darker now and as we looked at that bedraggled plane, now sitting in the shadows at the edge of the ramp. Someone felt sorry for the forlorn-looking thing and made some comment to that effect. We all had a good laugh at that.

Then he told us of the history of the Martin 404. It was one of the first small airplanes to replace the DC 3 after the war. The Martin Company had gained experience building bombers for the war and when the war ended, they designed a replacement for the DC 3. This plane had forty seats, was faster, and was more efficient to run. Delta had bought many of them for the intercity routes. The advent of the new small jet airplanes spelled the end of the Martin 404 and Delta sold their fleet to Southern Airlines. We then commented on Delta's good judgment and had a good laugh.

Fortunately, there were a few other people in the Lounge Area at that time so as boisterous as we were, we didn't upset anyone else in the lounge area. Our good mood was dissipating as the time dragged on and no new airplanes landed. It was getting close to what should have been our boarding time and we were wondering if we should start heading to the boarding area. We were certain that our plane should be landing soon, and we wanted to be ready.

At about this time, one of those little tugs roared to life and we watched as it drove through the snow heading toward that bedraggled-looking airplane. Then it hooked up to the front landing gear and began to tow it toward the terminal. I looked at my ticket which had been purchased through Delta and for the first time, I noticed that my Southern Airlines connection listed Martin 404 in the equipment section of my ticket. I mentioned this and suddenly we had a lot more respect for the little plane we had been making fun of.

We went to the gate and in due time boarded the plane. These were the days before most smaller planes were using jet ways to board through the front door. At this time, you walked out of the terminal on the tarmac to the plane and climbed the steps that were part of the plane at the front door. To make this possible, the plane had a boarding stairway that stored under the front door. This plane also had a boarding stairway that dropped down at the back of the plane. This allowed you to board using the steps at the tail. This was much easier than boarding at the front of the plane.

There were not many passengers on this flight, so the boarding went very fast. The plane had been sitting out in the cold and wasn't very warm when we boarded. This wasn't much of a problem for us salesmen as we were pretty *happy* and the *antifreeze* in our systems pretty much protected us from the cold.

I think that Southern had some means of blowing warm air into the cabin when the plane was first brought to the gate, but it was not very effective. There were other passengers in addition to our rowdy group and some did comment on how cold it was in the plane. We were met by a very young stewardess (that was what they were called back then) who welcomed us to the flight, the back door was closed, and we were ready for the flight.

The stewardess got us all settled down in our seats, checked to make sure we were buckled in and read the safety instructions for the flight. If I remember it right, it was at this point when the pilot began cranking the left engine. It turned over and as each piston came up in the cylinder, it made a sound like *rurr, rurr, rurr, rurr, rurr* and nothing happened.

At this point, he began to crank the right engine and as the first piston came up and it went *rurr*, one of the salesmen in front of me made a kind of grunting sound as though he was trying to help it along. This caught on with the rest of us and as the second piston came up and made the *rurr* sound we all chimed in.

This happened each time as several more pistons came up and made the *rurr* sound. The next piston came up and fired sending what appeared to be a flame shooting back from the engine. Most of us saw this and for some reason most of us gave a big cheer. Now that the engine was running smoothly I think we were encouraged.

Then the pilot began cranking the left engine again. When each piston came up and made the *rurr* sound, we then again tried to encourage it by making the noise. It started with a bang and again we began to cheer. We then quieted down, and the young stewardess made her last seatback and seat belt check and buckled herself into her seat. The plane taxied to the runway and setup for the takeoff roll. By this time, it seemed as though it was snowing pretty heavy and someone commented about that.

When you begin the takeoff roll in a jet plane the power is applied, and the jets spool up to full power and the resulting thrust usually is felt as you feel like you are being pushed back into your seat. This is not as noticeable in a radial engine powered plane, so as the power was applied and we began our slow takeoff roll, someone began to encourage the plane forward. From up the aisle, in about the middle of the plane, came this soft voice. Starting off quietly but getting louder repeating go, go, go and soon another voice chimed in. Soon most of us were encouraging the plane to become airborne by repeating *Go, Go, Go* until the plane had reached a pretty good altitude.

Usually, this would be the time for the stewardess to come by and take drink orders. In this case, as soon as it was safe, the young stewardess unbuckled herself from her seat and walked to the front of the plane not to be seen again until we approached Nashville. Soon thereafter, one of the pilots walked down the aisle to the back of the plane, turned around and walked slowly back to the front. We landed without any incident in Nashville, and most of the salesmen and some of the other passengers got off.

"The flight from Nashville to Memphis was so dull if I remembered it right. I slept."

When he had completed his story, we sat around with our coffee cups pondering the changes in air travel. Today, when that plane landed in Nashville, the whole group of salesmen would have been arrested for disorderly conduct or not obeying the instructions or *commands* of the flight attendant. We all agreed that today those salesmen might have exhibited attitudes or actions and not have been allowed on the plane in the first place.

When we left, we wished the friend who was going to Milwaukee a safe and boring flight.

The Bar Fight in Tennessee

Our old salesman's group was sitting around the table in the coffee shop the other day telling "War Stories" when we were interrupted. One person from our group received a phone call on his up-to-date cellphone. Naturally, it interrupted what we were talking about. We all jumped on him about how discourteous this was to have that "thing" inconveniently disrupt such a world-shattering conversation as we were having.

This brought other comments as to how communications have changed. One person in our group began to tell us about a time he needed to make a phone call.

It was in the late 1970s and he was on one of his usual sales routes through Eastern Tennessee. His inside salesperson had tracked him down by calling the companies he was to visit that day with an urgent message to call in immediately. He picked up this message on his second call of the day.

He called in to the home office as soon as he arrived at this customer's plant and picked up his message. One of his largest customers was having a problem with the equipment he had sold them. The problem was so bad that the customer's manufacturing process was shut down. He completed his call and dropped everything else he was planning for the day. He found a pay phone and placed a hurried call to the customer's plant telling them he was on the way.

He immediately drove several hours to visit the plant and solve the problem.

He recognized what the problem was as soon as he arrived. It was a warranty problem affecting a part supplied to his company by one of the vendors. It wasn't a big part and its shipment could be easily rushed. He got everything set in motion to have the part sent to the plant as soon as possible. If everything he had set up worked, the part would arrive in time to resume production at the beginning of second shift. There was nothing more he could do, so he left the factory and continued on his way to begin working on the next day's schedule.

He was about an hour from the plant, about halfway between Knoxville and Chattanooga, when he realized that he had made a serious mistake on the rush order he had called into the factory. He had neglected to add a necessary bracket needed for this part to be mounted as a replacement for the one that had failed.

He had to contact the factory and make the correction before the parts order would be taken to the airport by courier and put on the airplane which would be met by a courier and delivered, at great company expense, to his customer. Not only would the part be unusable until the bracket could be shipped, but the whole thing would make the company look bad and cost the customer more lost production time.

He exited I-75 at the entrance to a little town to look for a pay phone. In those days, pay phones were very common in the larger cities and some smaller towns, but not very common in the country. Usually, there would be a filling station that would have one, but not always. Sometimes, there would be a blue rectangular sign with the word *TELEPHONE* printed in white indicating that there was a phone nearby. In this case, there was a little store filling station by the side of the road with several cars and light trucks parked in front. He saw the *TELEPHONE* sign and decided to stop there.

He parked on the side of the building so he would be out of the way of any traffic that might come for the gas pumps. He got out of the car, locked it, and went inside. This was a *"little store"*. He entered the door into a very small room.

On one wall, was a rack holding a minimum display of groceries, candies, and the like. In the center, a pool table was shoehorned in with a minimal amount of space around it making cuing up a ball seem like a great challenge. On the back wall, was a bar with seven stools and a brass spittoon. Over on one-side wall, near the sign that indicated there were restrooms, hung a pay phone.

He entered, and a man standing behind the bar near the cash register welcomed him. The three men, in what looked like work clothes, standing at the bar talking and drinking acknowledged his presence. Immediately, he felt over dressed and out of place in his suit and tie. He asked if he could use the phone and the bartender nodded and pointed to where the phone hung on the wall.

He went to the phone and placed the necessary call to his inside salesperson and began to explain why he had called. She told him to hang on the line and she would track down where the order was and if it had been picked up by the courier yet. As he was standing there, handheld receiver piece to his ear, talking to the inside salesperson, a fight broke out amongst the men standing at the bar.

One picked up a pool queue and began heading toward one of the other men, who at that time was retreating toward the phone. Naturally, along with this there was a quite a bit of shouting and the repeating of some very *"salty"* language.

It was at that point that the salesman asked the inside salesperson on the phone to excuse him for a moment. He told her that he would be right back. He let the phone hand piece dangle from its stainless-steel cord beneath the black cast aluminum pay phone body and hastily retreated into the men's restroom. He waited there until the noise level indicated the fight must have ended. He then returned to finish his phone conversation.

When he explained to the inside salesperson what had just taken place she had a good laugh. She told him she wondered what all the commotion was all about, but dutifully waited for his return. It turned out that the courier had already picked up the part and was at the airport, but the call really wasn't necessary as the person in the parts department now automatically added the extra bracket to any order for that part. It seems that this warranty problem had come up before with another customer and the factory learned from that fiasco.

We all had a good laugh about how things used to be and that how rare it is now to find any coin-operated pay phone working at any place. One person from the group looked at the clock and commented that he was late to meet his wife.

Then as if someone had said,

"Start."

We each picked up our own cell phones and reported to someone that we were late.

Airplane Flu

You asked me a question about how a traveling man remains healthy when he is constantly exposed to whatever bacteria and viruses which are popular at any given time. What affected the traveling man also seemed to affect the people working in the airline industry. All who travel have had to face this dilemma and all have handled it differently. Let me tell you a story.

Back in the days, Eastern Airlines was one of the largest airline companies with many flights in and out of Atlanta; they were my favorite air carrier. I flew them so often that I earned a Gold Frequent Flyer designation. In time, I will explain to you what could be done with a Gold Card, but not now.

It was back in 1979, if my memory serves me correctly, that I had a major distributor for my products in Dallas, Texas. This distributor was so important that I would visit his facility at least every six weeks, if not, once a month. The flights I took were generally the same times and same numbers when I made those trips. My favorite place in the plane was in the back, usually in one of the last two rows, an aisle seat if I could get it.

The Atlanta-based stewardesses bidding these trips had enough seniority that they became regulars. Over the months, several other salesmen and I, who made the same trip regularly, got to know them quite well. It wasn't unusual that when all the passengers had been served and things quieted down that the stewardesses would join us at the back of the plane for some subdued levity. We would joke around with them and depending on the trip, it could have been perceived that we were actually having a party back there.

In those days, flying was so much different. The planes were smaller, the Federal rules were not as tight, and the whole atmosphere was different. There were two types of people who flew then, the first types were the Salesmen or the Businessmen who were regulars and very relaxed. The second types of people, the vast majority, were those who were somewhat fearful about flying. Some even occasionally used the "Air Sickness Bags" that were prominently displayed in the seat pocket in every row of seats.

The fall of that year was visited by a virulent strain of the flu. This flu would come upon you with about five minutes' warning after which you would begin to sweat, become dizzy, and sometimes throw up. It would usually pass within twenty-four to thirty-six hours. I mention this because this plays a critical part in the flight from Dallas to Atlanta one Thursday evening.

This flight began on Thursday afternoon, the week before Thanksgiving. I had an amazing week with them as everyone at the distributor's facility was looking forward toward the short work week ahead. My spirits were high. I was looking forward to getting back to Atlanta and finishing the week off early on Friday afternoon so I also could enjoy a short week in my office.

I turned in my Hertz rental car at the Dallas airport and was one of the last to board the plane. It was a dinner flight and I believe it was scheduled to leave at 5:30 p.m. I got to my seat and stowed my briefcase under the seat in front of me. I was second row from the back, aisle seat, just where I liked to ride. The stewardess was one who I had ridden with many times, and she gave me a cordial greeting.

The other stewardess came down the aisle and started doing the seat belt check. Several of the regulars were seated in their regular seats also. This looked like it would be a usual trip, and unless one of the other fellows was wound up and in a party mood this would be a dull trip. I think we were all tired and looking forward to the upcoming short week. Everything was in order for the flight to leave the gate, so the doors were shut, and we were pushed from the gate.

As we were being pushed back from the gate, one of the stewardesses spoke to the other in a kind of hushed voice.

"I think I'm coming down with the flu! I'm dizzy. Should we tell the pilot and go back to the gate?"

"No! I am feeling a little bad myself, but do we want to be stuck here for two days? We can do this!" the second stewardess said.

At that time, the FAA had a rule that a flight could not leave the gate without a full flight crew. If the plane would have returned to the gate the two stewardesses would have been relieved from duty. The plane would have had to remain at the gate until two other stewardesses could be found, or the flight would have had to be cancelled. This was Dallas and the chances that two other stewardesses could be found was slim to none.

If that had happened, we would all have had to rebook and some of us might have to wait until morning to fly home. It was obvious that these ladies wanted to get home. I believe the statement, *"We can do this!"* was as much of a relief for the several other frequent travelers, who probably also heard what they had said, as it was to me. I think we were all happy that these ladies didn't ask to go back to the gate.

They buckled themselves into their jump seats and in minutes we were air born. A little bit later the curtain separating first class from coach was pulled across the aisle and the flight had officially begun.

The first action the stewardesses took after takeoff for a dinner flight, such as this, was the unleashing of the drink cart. It became apparent to two of the regular riders that the stewardesses were having trouble with the drink cart. One appeared so dizzy she could hardly stand up. These two regulars got out of their seats and went up to where the stewardesses were working.

In a kidding manner, they made a challenge to the two stewardesses that they could do a better job. The stewardesses joked with them and soon, were supervising the two regulars who had in essence commandeered the drink cart. The way they clowned was very entertaining and soon the passengers in coach were in a party mood.

The drink cart finally made it back to the rear of the plane and was stowed. The two regulars were still clowning around. One of the stewardesses pretty much collapsed into the jump seat while the other one looked green around the gills.

One of the regulars went to the back and stood next to her,

"What are you planning to do about the dinners?" he asked.

I watched as she leaned against the bathroom door post and answered,

"I have no idea!"

"If we bring you the trays, can you serve them?" he asked.

"Yes, I think we can do that."

I don't remember what the stewardess in first class was doing or if she even was aware of what was happening in the coach section of the plane. She was probably so busy in first class she had no time to check. After a little conference in the back, it was decided that the one stewardess would serve the plates at the seats while the other would prepare the plates in the back. This required her to remove the trays from the racks in the catered food carts, then remove the aluminum foil covering it and place the cups and silverware on the tray.

The two regulars from the drink cart were still clowning around entertaining the passengers. They would bring the plates forward and the stewardess would serve them. This worked fairly well, but it was slower than usual because of all the clowning that took place.

All the meals were served, but the time was running out. We were fast approaching Atlanta. The flight had gone well, and we were ahead of schedule. The pilot announced that due to upper winds we would arrive ten minutes early. Again, Federal Air Regulations kicked in. All the food trays had to be gathered and properly stowed before landing. By this time, one stewardess was sitting in one of the seats of the regulars fast asleep. The two regulars jumped into action and began collecting the trays. The other stewardess began the process of separating the items from the plates and properly stowing them.

The way the regulars were working there was a need for someone to help. I brought the trays the last few steps to the stewardess who was sorting and stowing them. The trays were coming back so fast that in her condition, she had trouble keeping up with the flow. Also, in her condition, she was unable to bend over without becoming dizzy, so she sat down on the floor in front of the open doors of the catered food carts and the racks that she needed to stow the trays in.

All the trays were at the back, but some were still in a pile beside the stewardess, who from a sitting position on the floor, was frantically stuffing trays into the slots before her. Looking toward, the front of the plane, I saw the curtain being pulled open for landing. Then a voice was heard from the front of the plane telling us to fasten our seat belts, stow our tray tables, and to make sure our seat were in the full, upright position for landing.

Nobody did the seatbelt check or walk through making sure we had complied with the previous instructions. I was now in my seat safely belted in and looking back at the stewardess sitting on the floor of the galley still stuffing trays into the appropriate slots. One of the regulars was in the jump seat. One stewardess was asleep in the regular's seat while the other was still on the floor of the galley. She did get the doors to the catered food carts closed before we landed. The galley was ready for the cleanup crew. We landed and taxied to the gate. As soon as we stopped, even before the cabin door was opened the passengers were up and opening the bins to remove their carryon luggage. It seemed as though all were in a good mood and soon the plane was empty. Almost immediately, the galley door was opened and the food crew was removing the catered food carts and replacing them with the ones for the next flight. By this time, the two stewardesses were finishing their duties and getting ready to deplane. We came in early and I also made it home early.

The next time I saw one of those stewardesses was weeks later. We greeted each other cordially, but nothing was ever mentioned of our unusual flight. As I think back on my early days of flying, I am amazed at how free it was and the things that took place in the air. Flying used to be fun.

I often wonder how many of the passengers from that flight came down with that version of the flu. I didn't, but I had had probably been exposed sometime earlier and had a light case. In any case, I believe that we, traveling men, were exposed to so much that it took something really potent to take us down. I suppose this still holds true today.

The Divorced Salesman

I had signed up a new distributor in a large Midwestern city and was introduced to the sales force that would be selling my product. My product was a type of capital equipment used in manufacturing plants, and at other times, was used as a component of a manufactured product. The introduction went well, and I made note of everyone I would be training and working with.

The first man I met was Bill. He was an older man in his late forties, with short, balding dark hair, somewhat plump, and wearing glasses. He impressed me as the type of *"Good Old Boy"* salesman, laid back, and effective. He had sold a competitor's line and told me that he had always respected my product line and was looking forward to being able to sell the products. He gave me a hearty handshake.

The next person was Lucy. She was in her mid-thirties a tall, thin, brunette with riveting eyes. She impressed me by being efficient and in control. She worked mostly on phone sales but also had an outside territory. I would have to visit customers with her when necessary. She had never sold my products and would have to learn the line from the bottom up. She assured me that she had already studied my product line and was excited to get started with it. Her hand shake was very aggressive for that of a woman.

The third person was Henry. He was a tall, muscular, well-groomed man, black hair with no strand out of place, about forty with a very engaging smile. He had never sold my type of product, although most of his customers used this type of product. When he shook my hand, it was as though he gave me an electric shock.

The fourth person on the team was Carl. A young man, thin, crew cut, blond hair with an outgoing personality. He was just out of engineering school. He was what we used to call *"wet behind the ears"*. He was in training handling part orders and mostly older accounts. His handshake was awkward and not reassuring.

We sat around a table and I passed out the product catalogs to introduce them to the product line. I had to do very little to introduce the line as Bill jumped right in and began to share some of his experience with the applications. His personal testimony about our products was almost riveting. You can't buy that type of enthusiasm. All in all, we had a good first *get-to-know-you* meeting. Later, when talking with the owner, I learned that when the idea of taking on the line that I represented came up, it was Bill who tipped the scale in my favor.

When I work with a distributor, I plan my time to work *"on a one to one"* basis with each salesperson. I have found that this is the best way to make sure that each is comfortable with the product line. It helps to give each person confidence in the product. It also helps each person know when to contact me for technical help, if needed, with the sale. It is when making end-user calls in the territory with each salesperson that I have the opportunity to know each of them better. I encourage them to plan a full day of making calls, but I make it a practice to get them back to the distributor's office at quitting time, so they can go home and spend the evening with their family. When we work together on calls, I usually pick up lunch. Occasionally, I will take a group out for an evening meal, but that must be a special occasion.

When we were not talking about the product, Bill would tell me about his wife and the quilting she was doing for their kids. Lucy had three young ones at home, and I heard about their antics. Henry was rather silent about his private life and concentrated on learning the technical aspects of the product and we talked of little else. Carl was into sports, and I really envied his high energy level and physical stamina.

During the first year that I worked with them, the company sales of my product line was good. Not just good, but it went *through the roof.* In honor of the great year we had just experienced and as an incentive for the next year, I invited the owner and the sales staff to a night at a famous restaurant in the city.

The invitation was for the salespeople and their immediate family. I met Bill's wife and talked about quilts. I met Lucy's husband and the kids that I had heard so much about. I also met Carl's fiancé. I was surprised that Henry came alone. I thought I finally might meet the person I had heard nothing about and to whom I expected that he went home to each night.

It was several weeks later that we were scheduled to work together again. This was a high dollar sale and he wanted to make the best proposal and presentation he could. He seemed nervous about this job, so he invited me to work up the proposal with him and be a part of the presentation.

He had set two days out of his usual schedule to do this. For two days, we would work closely together and burn the midnight oil. He asked me if I could meet him the night before we would sit down in the office to work on the proposal. I agreed to meet him at his house that evening at 6:00 p.m. I thought this to be strange, but strange things happen sometimes in my world.

I located his apartment building. It was an older three story, shabby-looking, red brick building in a less affluent part of the city. I opened the door to the entrance hall lit by one light bulb hanging on a cord from the ceiling. I climbed the unlighted stairs to the second-floor landing which was also lighted by a single bulb hanging on a cord from the ceiling. Again, I climbed the unlit stairs to the third-floor landing also lighted by a single bulb. I found his door and knocked on it.

He responded, "Come in, the door is not locked."

I opened the door and went in. I didn't know what I was expecting, but what I saw was a shock. He seemed to be doing well selling the products he represented and certainly did very well selling mine, yet I opened the door to an almost bare two room apartment. In it was a kitchenette, a kitchen table with two chairs, a couch with an end table and lamp. There was a TV against the wall across from the couch, and a small radio on a small bookcase next to it.

From what I saw, the books in the bookcase were sales manuals for the products he sells. Next to the radio was a picture frame with what looked like a picture of four young children. There were curtains on the window near the TV and on the window by the kitchenette. The half open door to the bathroom was next to the kitchenette.

This combination living room / kitchen looked sterile; the dark wood floor was bare. The walls were painted beige and had several landscape pictures hanging on them. The ceiling was painted white. From what I could see of the bedroom, it looked just as sterile.

Henry came out of the bedroom, gave me a welcoming handshake.

"I'm so glad you could come by tonight. I really wanted to work with you in a less pressured environment to start this off."

He ushered me into the kitchenette, pulled out a kitchen chair from the table, and offered it to me. He walked over to the sink, opened a cupboard door, took two coffee cups from the shelf, and asked if I wanted tea or coffee. I took coffee which he warmed in the microwave that was positioned on the counter by the sink, and brought to me. He then filled his cup with tea from a pot on the stove and sat down at the table across from me.

He looked down at the drink in his cup as though it could help him arrange his words in such a way that they would make sense when he spoke them.

"You know I have only been with this company for about three years," he stated.

"Yes, the owner told me when he took my line that you were new at this," I replied.

"Did he tell you that I had never sold capital equipment before? That I sold men's clothing? Or that I moved here from a city 200 miles from here?" he nervously asked.

"No, he only said that you were a fast-learner and a hard worker. I thought that was high praise," I responded.

"The reason I wanted to meet with you was to understand the process we will be going through to put that proposal together tomorrow. I have never put together a proposal this complicated before. Normally, when I must do something that I am unfamiliar with, Bill will jump in and give me hints and advice. Lucy has been very helpful with proposal layouts and things of that nature. This project however is the largest and most complicated I have ever had the opportunity to quote. I can't count on help from Bill, Lucy, or Carl on one this complicated, and I don't want the owner to have to step in and help on this. I don't want him to know just how much I don't know. I suspect he will be involved with this at closing, but I want to be the one to bring it to that point," he concluded.

"How did you come to make the jump from selling men's clothing to selling capital equipment?" I asked.

"It is a long story. I was a partner in a men's clothing store in the town I was from. I was married, well technically, I probably still am. That is why this job is so important to me. It is an opportunity to get out of debt faster," Henry explained.

What he had said didn't make a whole lot of sense, and he didn't explain any anything more. The little that he shared was now beginning to make some sense, his immaculate appearance, him never mentioning his family, and sparse living arrangements. I pondered his statement for several moments and did not reply right away. I don't know what he read from my actions, but he jumped in and immediately changed the subject.

He opened a notebook and took the actions that a college student would take if he were in a classroom lecture hall waiting to hear some very important lecture.

"Can you give me an outline of how we will begin to put together the proposal so that I look like I know what I am doing when we work together tomorrow?"

We worked at his kitchen table until about 9:30 when I had suggested to him that he had a good grasp as to what we would be doing in the morning. I suggested we might start a little earlier, but he said 8:00 a. m. would be the best. Later I found out that, when he wasn't traveling in his territory, he attended morning Mass at the local Catholic Church which was why 8:00 was his best time to start work.

On my way to my motel, I began to wonder how a man living in his drab surroundings could be the same man that had been so cheerful and outgoing when we worked together during the past year. I didn't see anything in his apartment that wasn't work-related. *"How can anyone live like that?"* I wondered.

The next day we worked out the details of the proposal to make it conform to the engineering specifications. We had the proposal formatted. The things we lacked to complete it were the details that would be faxed to the office the next day from my company.

"Henry, we just put in a good day's work and I am hungry, what are your plans for dinner tonight?" I asked at quitting time.

"I plan to go home, fix something to eat, study the proposal, and go to bed," he answered.

"We have worked hard all day on this, why don't you join me for a relaxing dinner where we can just get to know each other better?" I asked.

I really wanted to find out more about his background. That information could come in handy as we worked as a team during the presentation. I didn't want to be blindsided by something from his past which might come up during the presentation, or later during any negotiations that might follow.

"Yeah, that would be good. I might be able to relax a little," he replied.

"Do you know a good place to go?"

"There is a barbeque place close by, the food is usually pretty good," he replied.

We drove there in separate cars. Once inside, we settled on a table and went up to the counter and ordered our meals. I found it interesting that Henry chose to come to such a simple place. I had expected to go to some bar or lounge-type establishment where we could eat and talk over a bottle of beer or a glass of wine.

I always find the salespeople that I work with tend to become more relaxed in a dimly lit bar or lounge and after a beer or two tend to talk more freely. Considering the place he chose, I didn't expect to find out a lot about him this night.

When our numbers were called, we went to the counter, picked up and paid for the food, and got settled at a table to eat. I commented on the food and the brightness of the place. We talked about the weather and some other things, mostly small talk.

Finally, I asked the question that was really the reason I wanted to learn more about him,

"Why did you give up your men's wear store? Move away from your home and come here and choose to sell capital equipment?"

"It is a long story," he said as he looked down at his plate and kind of shook his head, "It's a long story".

We talked some more, but he didn't tell me anymore about his past. It was getting late, so we decided to call it a night and I headed back to my motel. This night he seemed more depressed. From what he said and his resigned attitude, I began to sense a certain loneliness about him, a melancholy that slowly overcame the evening. So far, he never indicated that he had a social life away from his work. There was no mention of a current girlfriend.

When he came in for work, he was in a good mood. None of the melancholy from last night was there. About 10:00 a.m., my company faxed the last of the critical performance data. Around noon, the final pricing we needed came in. We now typed up the final proposal and began the proof reading.

We then practiced the presentation until Henry felt comfortable with answering the technical questions that we expected to get. We decided to call it a day. And at quitting time, I asked Henry if he wanted to go out again to eat.

This time, I chose the spot. A nice, quiet neighborhood bar, near my motel. One that I had occasionally used when I was in town in the past. The atmosphere was that of a laidback sports bar. It had a TV with the sound turned down in one corner, and you could choose to sit far enough from it that the sound wouldn't bother you.

The menu was broad enough to include everything from burgers to a nice-sized steak dinner. The lighting was bright enough to read the menu but subdued enough to be relaxing. The drink menu included everything from wine to beer, and even soft drinks. The tables were round and small, and the chairs were padded and on casters. The whole atmosphere was one that encouraged you to leave your cares at the door and relax.

We arrived at the place in separate cars. I went in and found a table at the back, in the corner, away from most of the activity. Henry came in and joined me. The waiter came over to give us our menus and take our drink order. I ordered a glass of wine; Henry ordered a Coke.

"What is good here?" asked Henry.

"I normally get the half rack of rib plate," I answered.

"Then I'll get the same," Henry responded.

The waiter returned with our drinks and we placed our order.

We talked a little about sports. He pointed out how well the Notre Dame Football team was doing. I countered with how well my Alma Matter had done last week. I broke the ice with some of the things I had planned for the coming weekend. This brought us around to a little discussion about family. I told him about my son who was away at college and was a cheerleader. He mentioned that his four kids were all playing sports. This brought our conversation around to other family things. The food came, then we ate and talked more about family. He was opening up to me and began to tell me a little about how he came to be in this city.

He began,

"After high school I went to Notre Dame. I was a good faithful Catholic and in my freshman year even considered going into the priesthood. That idea got pushed to the side when I met this girl. She also was in the business school studying Advertising. We studied together for some of the classes and after graduation, I proposed. We were married in her home church."

"After the wedding, we settled down in her hometown. She got a job in advertising right away, so we were financially stable. I was unable to find a job right away. I had a couple of friends from college that couldn't find jobs right away either. We looked over the market and saw a need for a high-end men's store. With loans, we were able to start that high-end men's store."

"The store was very successful, and she was doing very well in the advertising world. We decided it was time, so we bought this big old house at a good price in the better part of town. I still own half of that house and still pay the mortgage. We, being good Catholics, practiced rhythm method of birth control and low and behold after we got settled in that house the first of our children were born, a boy."

"He sure changed the routine around the house. Her job in advertising was going well and the store was doing good, and we were very happy. We decided for a babysitter and she went back to work. Then one night at dinner, she announced that she had missed a period and might be pregnant again. She was very upset over this. Her job had been going so good and she wanted to work a couple more years before we had our next child."

"After the second child was born, she tried to work, but it became too much. The income from the store was good enough so she could become a stay-at-home mom and that was how it went. We had two more children. She had wanted a girl, but we ended up with four boys."

"About the time the fourth child started school, she became restless and went back to work. That didn't work out so well, so we divorced, and I moved 200 miles away. I still pay child support, but I don't see my kids."

With that his melancholy returned, he just looked down at the table and sighed.

"We should probably call it a night," I suggested.

"Yah, I need to be good and ready for tomorrow's presentation."

We left and I had the hope that he would be over his melancholy and be bright and cheery in the morning.

The next day, he came in to work cheery with no hint of how his attitude was the night before. As we drove to our important presentation, he practiced the presentation with me. When we arrived, he made the presentation and we got a commitment for the project and our first order. This turned out to be, over a long period of time, a number of orders, and a whole new range of product applications opened up. The account would become much bigger than it originally appeared. I would be working closely with this salesman on this account for a long time.

As we worked together, we became very close and one night he opened to me about his situation. His story was a sad, but not an unusual one. I have heard many variations of it. I knew he was divorced, but after that night I found out, out of respect, had never broached the subject again. After one of the successful presentations to our special customer, we went out to eat at a bar close to the distributor's office.

That night, he had a glass of wine along with his dinner. He got his wallet out and tried to pay for the meal, but I used my usual approach and said,

"I called the meeting, so I pick up the check," and paid the bill.

His wallet lay open on the table and he just looked at a picture in it. From what I could see in the dim light, it was of a beautiful woman surrounded by four lovely children. He noticed that I had seen the picture and kind of blushed. I looked away, but he didn't try to hide the picture either.

After a long silence he stated,

"This is my ex-wife and my four boys. It was taken before the divorce."

"Oh," I embarrassedly responded, "I didn't mean to intrude."

He apologetically said,

"Everyone I work with knows I am divorced, but I have kept pretty much to myself. I was married and the Catholic Church does not recognize divorce. Being a faithful Catholic makes it very difficult."

He was finally opening up with me. I didn't know how to respond, so I sat in silence trying to think of a response.

A good salesman abhors silence, so Henry spoke to fill the gap,

"When the children got older, she became restless and wanted to go back into advertising. She sent out resumes and, because of her degree and past experience, she was offered the position of Assistant to the President. This began as more or less a glorified secretarial position, but as time went on, her background and her degree impressed the President and her duties were expanded."

"She became necessary at all the large corporate meetings which sometime took place after business hours and on weekends. I was busy with my clothing business and could not always be there for the children. This conflicted with her increased travel. She started to be away so often that we hired a nanny to take care for the children when she was gone."

"This went on for about a year. At her next company review, she received a rather large raise and more responsibility. This meant she traveled with the President to more conferences and was away for a couple of weeks at a time in some instances."

"When all of her traveling began, a problem arose. Being that we were faithful practicing Catholics, we practiced the rhythm method of birth control. With my work schedule and her travel schedule, we didn't have time alone together when she was in the safe time of her cycle."

"This led to much frustration on my part and many long *'discussions'*. We were losing the closeness that most married couples share. I felt my marriage was coming apart and there was nothing I could do about it. We hadn't made love for six months, it was not that I didn't try, but she never knew where she was in her cycle. With her traveling so much, she claimed it wasn't predictable. As a practicing Catholic she refused to use any birth control options. She had achieved such a great, *high paying* position in the agency that she decided that making love with me was too dangerous."

"I suggested we get marriage counseling. We talked to a priest. He laid out the Church's position. Then we went to a Marriage Counselor the priest recommended. After more discussion and counseling about what marriage was and what was expected of a husband and wife in a good marriage, she decided that we would sleep in separate bedrooms. She didn't consult me she just decided. She made arrangements for me to stay at a nearby motel until another bedroom could be added to the back of the house for my use.""At this point, I moved out of the house, and to save money got a cheap apartment on the other side of town. We continued to go to counseling, but things didn't change, and no new bedroom was added to the house."

"This turmoil was having an effect on the kids. The nanny became a permanent resident in the house, and I was basically shut out. My partners tried their best to help with my work schedule, but it was difficult for me to come over to the house to do things at night with the kids. She decided that she didn't want me to come over to the house when she wasn't there and visit the kids. 'She claimed it was too disruptive!' There were only limited times she would be free for me to come and visit the kids. My apartment was too small for the kids to come over and visit. This was not working out. I complained."

"It was at this point, when I went to the next counseling session, when I was presented with legal separation papers. I immediately got a lawyer to fight this and we went to court. The separation papers led to her filing the divorce papers."

"During the court proceedings, it became apparent that she had something going on with her boss. These things tend to come out when good lawyers get involved. There was a long drawn out fight which included charges of infidelity and it became nasty."

"A divorce was granted to her. I ended up being responsible for the house which I still own half of, and I pay the taxes on. I pay child support until they are eighteen years old. The kids live with their mother and I have been given the rights to visit them, but not at the house."

"According to the state I am legally divorced. According to the Catholic Church, I cannot remarry until we get our marriage annulled. Because of the circumstances, an annulment is very unlikely."

"I sold my share of the business to cover the legal bills and pay off some of the mortgage on the house. I moved away due to the rancor left over from the divorce. That's why I am here, 200 miles away from my kids. Now you know my story." He finished sitting there in silence.

I didn't know what to say. He had told me his story and I had to respond,

"How often do you get home to see the kids?"

"Now that we are doing so much business with the new company, I have been able to go back twice. I get a motel room and they come over," he replied.

We talked far into the night and I learned a lot of things about this remarkable man. The reason that we can't usually begin work before 8:00 in the morning is that he faithfully attends early Mass and that ends in time to be at work at 8:00. He credits his faith and his daily attendance at Mass for giving him the strength he needs to face each new day. He rarely drinks an alcohol beverage at night because he doesn't want alcohol to drown his sorrows and turn him into a drunkard.

His Catholic Church has begun a weekly evening Christian Fellowship group for divorced men and women. This has given him some social outlet other than work. He has had some civil contact lately with his ex concerning the kids and is hopeful this will lead to a closer relationship with them.

That account was a part of my territory for several more years, but as with any sales territory, things change, and I was moved to another territory. We do keep in touch at Christmas though and he writes that he has been very successful.

Over the years, I have worked with many divorced salesmen and heard many stories. The common perception of the traveling salesman is that of a carousing, party-loving person of low morals. This may have been the case for a few of them, who because of their antics, stood out in a crowd, but for the most part, the salesmen work hard and long to support their families.

The divorced salesmen I have worked with over the years never saw it coming. While they were spending time away from home working, their wives found other things to do. Finally, when the time was right the wife left.

The DON

It happened when my territory included the coal country in Eastern Pennsylvania. What I did was to fly into the city that was nearest to where the distributor that I would be working with was located and rent a car to go visit. This is what brought me to Wilkesboro, PA where my very good distributor in the area was expanding his sales force. It was my practice to schedule a week wherein I could train a new hire on the products that my company manufactured. This training usually consists of a day of intense study of my products followed by two days of field sales training on how to sell.

I arrived on a Tuesday morning and after meeting with the owner, I was introduced to the new man. We spent the first day in the office and I went through the catalog pointing out the way the various products complimented the products he normally sells. We then took a long lunch break which I normally do for us have a better chance to get to know each other better.

During the lunch break, I found out that the young man I was training that week was twenty-two years old. He had completed two years at the local technical college and held a technical degree. He was of Italian descent and had grown up in the Wilkesboro area in a very Italian neighborhood.

He came from a family of coal miners who were very active in union affairs. He had a good background for the territory he was covering. I was impressed with how fast he learned what we had covered that morning.

That afternoon, we covered the servicing side of my company's product. This knowledge comes in handy when calling on engineers. I always make sure that my salesmen know when to tell the customer *"I don't know that, but I will get the answer for that and get back to you"*. The afternoon session went very well. The field training consisted of riding together to make sales calls on prospects, discussing the products in the catalogue as they applied to the various customer needs, and then physically making the sales calls. As my sales territory consisted of many states it would be some time before I could be back to work with the new salesperson again, so I had to get in as many sales calls with him as possible during the two days we had together.

To accomplish this, we would begin early in the morning and not get back to his office until late in the day. To get the most catalogue time in for the salesperson, I would drive my rental car and have him study the catalogue while riding with me. With me driving this meant that sometimes during the day I would have to pull to the side of the road and answer calls from my factory on the cellphone. It is important to note that the President of my company at this time was named Donald "Don" Rinalldi.

The first day that we traveled together, we left his office at 7:30; before I could check into my factory office for any early morning messages. It was about mid-morning and we were riding along, analyzing the results from the first two sales calls when my cell phone rang. I pulled off to the side of the road to answer the call.

It was the factory that was contacting me and instructing me to call Don Rinalldi as soon as it was convenient as he needed to discuss something with me. President Don Rinalldi didn't usually call me. Usually, someone in the Sales Department would be the one I would talk to. This must be a very big problem if he would take time out of his day to want to talk to me.

I steered the car from the shoulder of the road back into traffic and asked my rider if he knew of a convenient place along this road to pull off and park so I could make my call. He made a suggestion, and we parked in a parking spot in front of a quick stop. He was curious about the call and I explained that I had to make a call to Don Rinalldi to answer some questions about a problem. There was nothing concerning the call that would be confidential, so I made no effort to keep what I was doing confidential.

I called the factory using the secret 1-800 number that we in the sales department use and asked the operator to put me through to Don Rinalldi. Because of the background traffic I had the volume on my cell phone turned up. I was put through to the President's office and Don picked up the call.

We talked. Don pointed out to me that "I" had a credit problem with one of my distributors in another state and a large order would not ship until "I" straightened it out. We discussed the credit problem in some detail. Don pointed out the credit history we had with the distributor. Don was adamant that I pay a "collection call" on this distributor.

He even suggested that I *"lean"* on this distributor. It is possible that Don's urgent tone of voice was reflected in how I answered him. The call ended with me assuring Don that I would change my schedule and visit him to take care of the problem the next week. That was how the call ended.

I put the phone back in my pocket, looked over at my rider and asked him if he needed anything from the quick stop before we continued on our way. I noticed that he was sitting upright as if at attention and indicated that *"he didn't need a thing"*. I pulled out of the parking lot and we were on our way.

As I looked over at him, I noticed that his demeanor had changed. Before the phone call he seemed to be happy and carefree, but now he looked more defensive and reserve, maybe even scared. I tried to return to the conversation we were having before the interruption of the cell phone call, but *he* seemed as though he had lost the thread and was silent.

Alan M. Oberdeck

I brought up the next call we were to make. He was a little more responsive and we looked in the catalogue at the product that would solve the customer's problem. I went over the various ways we could pitch the product to the customer and reviewed with him how the product could save the prospect money by using it. He was still very reserve and somewhat nervous.

We stopped for lunch and I tried to break the ice. I thought discussing personal things such as family and kids would bring things back to normal. Touching on those kinds of things usually will lead to a more relaxed atmosphere. It did no good, he still appeared tense. The best way I could describe the conservation at lunch was guarded.

The first sales call after lunch was to deliver an engineering catalogue to an Engineering Firm. My young sales trainee handled it in a very professional manner. I told him I was impressed with his grasp of the product line. He thanked me for the praise, and we headed to our next sales call.

The next sales call was some distance away and would take about forty-five minutes to travel there. During this time, my trainee began to ask some very interesting questions, not about the product, but about the history of the company. As we rode, the questions became more pointed. He wanted to know when the company started.

I did my best to explain how the founder had invented a simple piece of machinery that would solve a problem for the company he worked for. It was that success that had other engineers asking him how to do the same thing. He quit his job and started building the product for other companies. Gradually, the product was the answer for other problems and the company grew.

He asked about ownership. I explained that the company was a closely-held. privately owned company, and that the ownership had no interest in a general stock offering.

He then asked about some of the employees. I told him that the president was of course Don Rinalldi, and he commented on that being an Italian name. I told him the name of the sales manager. I thought it would impress him that our service manager was named

Ken Ferrani which was an Italian name he could identify with. I also bragged about Joe, our best service tech who also was also of Italian descent. At that point, he became very nervous.

I looked over at him and asked if anything was wrong, and he assured me *"not a thing"*, but I knew something was not sitting right with him. From the way he was acting, I was concerned about even making the next sales call with him.

I decided that I had to get to the bottom of this and pulled into the next gas station we came to and parked the car. I turned to him and asked point blank what was wrong. He turned slightly white and asked me if I was *"connected"*. Now this threw me for a loop.

"Me? Connected? Where could he come up with an idea like that?" I pondered this for a minute or so, and decided the best approach was to be direct.

I looked him straight in the eye and asked him where he had gotten that idea. I had no idea what I might have said that could have led him to think that.

His answer made sense. He was second generation Italian and he *knew how things worked*. First, the company was family owned. Second, he assumed the family had Italian connections. Third, the company Service Manager had an Italian name and our chief tech had an Italian name. Fourthly, the company was run by a "DON".

Now it came to me. Since my phone call to Don Rinalldi this morning, this salesman had been worried that he has been riding with someone with mafia connections, selling a product made by a factory owned and run by the mafia.

It took some explaining to convince him that the president of the company I worked for was named Don as in *Donald* Rinalldi and bore the title of President, not DON. I explained that the city where my company was based had a lot of Italians living there and it would not be unusual to have people with Italian names in executive positions managing it.

After answering more of his questions and explaining more about the family that owned the company, he relaxed, and our relationship returned to how it was that morning. We got back to his office late and called it a day. Since he was single and I would have to eat alone, I asked him if he would pick a good Italian restaurant and have dinner with me; and we had a good meal.

We started work early the next day and things went well. We continued to work together as long as I covered that territory, and he still may be selling for that distributor.

Later after one of our Sales Meetings when we were relaxing at dinner, I had the opportunity to share this story with Don Rinalldi, and he had a good laugh.

The Comeuppance

Harold Lutz, the scourge of the Service Department, was coming out west to do a routine service analysis at the proving grounds near Yakama, Washington. This was in the early 1970s, and this was a new product, so our company wanted feedback on its operation. Because this was a new product, it was important that it was performing well. We got the announcement. The word from the factory was clear, that Harold be met by the Regional Manager, me, and Chris Dunham, the Special Accounts Manager for Yakama. Harold's schedule was clear. The two of us were ordered to meet him at Sea Tac Airport on Monday evening at 9:30 p.m. when his flight was scheduled to arrive.

Now there are a very few people that most good-natured sales types really dislike, but then there was Harold. He was 6 feet and 2 inches tall, muscular, blond headed with blue eyes. He was obviously born in the wrong era, to the right family, but the wrong country. This embodiment of a Prussian Military General was the most arrogant, self-centered, all-knowing person you ever really wanted to avoid.

No sales meeting was complete until the guys got together around a beer and listened to the newest telling of the newest *"Harold Lutz happening"*. The stories were never told from the podium. They were whispered in dark corners, retold in the quiet of the men's room, whispered from one salesman to another and alluded to in inside jokes, but never told by the speakers at meetings.

Alan M. Oberdeck

The last *Harold Lutz happening*, that I had heard about, took place in a diner in south western Pennsylvania. Harold, a new Factory Technician Trainee, and George Hendrix the Special Accounts Manager were having breakfast at a roadside diner. This was the local hangout filled with blue-collar types getting their breakfast before a strenuous day's work. As George told it, the place was full, five people to a four-chair-table full. Harold had ordered a very special twist to his scrambled eggs. George and the factory man each had a standard stack of pancakes. The order for the table was brought out and served.

Harold took one look at the dish, which looked perfectly good to us, and pointed out to the waitress all of the pickiest problems he had with what was served and how it differed from what he had asked for. He was unusually loud, and he really made a scene. The waitress took it well. The cook redid the order to the best of his ability. This time, he personally brought his creation out of the kitchen and placed it on the table for Harold's inspection. Harold inspected the plate, took out his notebook and began to write notes to the cook about how he could improve upon this creation on his plate.

By this time, many of the blue-collar types had, almost silently, moved from their tables and chairs and were gathered behind the cook, kind of collectively looking over his shoulders. George and the factory man had fortunately finished their pancakes. George had had begun to get out of his chair and signaled the factory man to do the same to get ready to leave. George, fortunately, was foresighted enough to leave enough money on the table to cover at least four meals and a healthy tip for the waitress.

Harold still sat there writing on his note pad, unknowing, or unconcerned about what was happening around him. Finally, as they all watched, Harold carefully pulled the paper from the pad, being careful not to let the paper tear anyplace but along the pre-stamped perforations. He looked up from the plate to the cook and began to read the list of improvements he wanted to make for the food to be *"edible"*.

The cook was very calm, like the calm before the storm. George and the factory man backed away from the table and snuck towards the door. The blue-collar types kind of circled the table like a pack of wolves circling a lone victim. As Harold read from his list, the cook's complexion took on a reddish hue.

Harold continued to read from his notes and point to things in the food on his plate. Finally, the cook had had enough. He reached down and picked up the plate from the table, took the list Harold handed him, and dumped the plate on Harold's head and then placed the list neatly on top. He nodded to the blue-collar types standing around the table and asked if they would be so kind as to expeditiously escort or remove Harold from the premises.

George and the factory man found Harold sitting in the dirt behind the diner wearing his breakfast. After renting another motel room for Harold to clean up in, and phoning the customer to change the arrival time, they went on the call.

George said he used to eat at that diner often but hasn't been back since.

As far as servicing the product goes, Harold is probably the best mechanic we have. He knows more about it, he is more meticulous, and he can repair a unit better than the engineers who designed it. When he is done, whatever the unit, it will perform better than when it was new.

Well, this is the Harold we are about to pick up. I am based in Los Angeles, so I flew up and arrived at Sea Tac at 7:25 p.m., and Chris met me at the gate. Now Chris and I have been working together for a long time, but I have never seen him look so happy. As I walked off the plane into the gate area, there he was smiling from ear to ear. We said our greetings and his voice sounded as though he was bursting at the seams to tell me something. We picked up my luggage and put it in his car.

Pry as I might, I couldn't find out from him what he was so excited about. Chris suggested we go and get a bite to eat before Harold arrives as he didn't want to have to change eating places quite yet, and we both laughed. I did find out Chris had us staying in the Holiday Inn, Boeing Field for the night. We would leave for Yakama in the morning. Over food, we discussed his territorial results and his plans for the next quarter, but I still had no idea what was making him so excited.

We met Harold in the baggage claim area and hurriedly went to the car and got in, Harold in the front and me in the back with his luggage. We left the airport in somewhat of a hurry and got out onto I-5 right away. I knew where the Holiday Inn Boeing Field was, and this was not the shortest way to get there. Harold began regaling us with what he felt was his latest fete of greatness, but I pretty much ignored him and didn't really listen.

We were heading north on I-5 right past the exit we should have taken west by Boeing Field. I wasn't lost, but I had no idea where we were heading. This certainly was not the way to our Holiday Inn. Harold was still telling how he reengineered this product in the field and how the engineers... Finally, Chris exited from I-5 and headed down into the valley.

"We must be close to the north end of Boeing Field," I thought.

Chris drove through back streets and suddenly, the engine of the car sputtered, coughed, and the car bounced to a sudden stop.

Harold was in his glory. He stopped telling his stories, exited the car, got the hood up, and had Chris crank the engine while he listened. For being stuck late at night in what appeared to be an unsavory part of town, Chris looked ecstatic. I followed Chris out of the car, and we joined Harold looking under the hood. Harold had the air cleaner off and was looking at the top of the carburetor explaining that the carburetor looked dirty and was probably at fault.

Suddenly Chris looked up, pointed, and yelled. I looked up and turned in panic to run because here, coming right down on top of us was this giant airplane dropping as though it were about to crash. It looked as though it were not more than thirty feet above us. Chris grabbed my arm and pulled me back. What I saw next was incredible, and I will try to explain it in the best way possible.

Harold looks up, sees the plane, bangs his head on the hood, looks up again, screams something about napalm, bumps his head again, and runs off in the direction the plane was coming from.

I turned and watched as the plane landed at Boeing Field. Chris put the air cleaner back on the carburetor, closed the hood with a bang, and got back in the car and started the engine. I got back into my spot in the back seat behind Chris, and he explained his anti-car-theft ignition switch to me. We began to look for Harold. Chris drove, and I walked the streets around the area. Where could he have gone? We called off the search at about 2:00 a.m. and went to claim our rooms at the motel.

I had now participated in the little plot Chris had cooked up to *get* Harold. The problem was we had *lost* Harold in the process. Harold was a big man; we knew he had to turn up someplace in the morning. We would just have to wait. Neither of us slept well that night.

At 6:00 a.m., I phoned the factory to pick up messages. I couldn't sleep so I might as well get an early start. My one and only message was that the company President, Dr. Cook wanted a word with me as soon as I called in. As the call was being transferred, I knew in my heart of hearts that President Dr. Cook was not going to have kind words for me, as he really didn't know me and I had only met him four times in my life.

While I hung there in that telephone limbo generously called hold, I tried to figure out what kind of a lie I could use to cover Chris and me. Before I could think of one, President Dr. Cook was on the line.

"What did you do to Harold?" he questioned.

"Where is Harold?" I asked in return.

I reasoned if he knew Harold was not with us, he might know where to find him.

"The Seattle police have him locked up in some Psycho Ward. They found him some time around 1:00 a.m. huddled in a ditch muttering something about the dry season, napalm, and the rice patties being mined."

"Where can I go to find him?" I reluctantly asked.

"I'll transfer you over to medical when I am through with you. What happened?"

Now I was on the spot. Chris and I were in real trouble. The best I could hope for was that Harold wouldn't remember, so I answered,

"He saw this big airplane and took off running from the car."

"I want to talk to him as soon as he is out!" finished President Dr. Cook.

Medical had everything straightened out so all we had to do was to go pick Harold up. I signed the papers and took a much-subdued Harold to the car. We went back to the Holiday Inn room where we again called back to the factory. President Dr. Cook talked to Harold. Harold in fact didn't remember anything at all about that night.

President Dr. Cook questioned each of us personally. He asked me to describe what took place. I told the truth, the car stalled near the end of the runway at Boeing field and Harold reacted to a landing plane. Then Chris got on the phone and talked with the President for some time. It was decided that instead of going in late we postpone our call to the next day.

Chris had had this stunt planned for about two weeks. His plan was as exact as anything Harold had ever planned. It was planned right down to the exact times of the scheduled freight planes coming into Boeing Field. This was planned only as a practical joke. This is one "Harold Lutz" story which will never be repeated at any sales meeting.

Fred and Ella

Dear Pastor Bob,

Last week my business took me out of town over the weekend. The job was scheduled to be completed by Friday afternoon, but there were complications and I had to stay Saturday until Monday to complete it. The person I was working with was Lutheran and knowing that I am Lutheran, he invited me to join him and his family on Sunday for church and later recreation. I felt honored that he asked, and I accepted his invitation.

At the beginning of the service, the pastor welcomed the visitors, recognized those members having birthdays during the week and those couples who were celebrating their wedding anniversaries. Among those celebrating were Fred and Ella who were celebrating their 60 years of marriage on Tuesday.

When the pastor had finished this routine announcement, he then issued an invitation on behalf of the church for all to stay after the service. The ladies of the congregation had organized a special potluck, sit-down dinner in honor of Fred and Ella's Anniversary. At that point, my host nudged me and whispered,

"We will be well fed."After the service, the whole congregation moved to the church basement where the festive atmosphere soon developed. There were several tables pushed together to form a long line where the potluck dishes of food were placed. At the end of the line was a three-tiered white frosted wedding cake, complete with bride and groom figures on top. The pastor looked at the food that was laid out and led the congregation in reciting in unison the Lutheran table prayer,

"Come, Lord Jesus, be our guest and let this food to us be blessed, Amen."

We all took a plate to go through the food line. Making his way through the crowd to the head of the line was the pastor, leading Fred who was pushing Ella in her wheelchair. This was the first time I had seen the pair. Fred was dressed in a dark suit and white shirt with a bright blue tie. He was tall, slim, and slightly hunched over.

He had the weathered face of one who had faced diversities and yet his face had a pleasant warm look about it. He was lovingly pushing Ella in her wheelchair. Ella wore a flower-printed dress with a white shawl wrapped around her shoulders. She was plump and fit, the perfect vision of what a grandmother should look like. Her white hair was curled and formed a halo around her smiling face.As he pushed her wheelchair in front of the tables of food, they worked together as a pair putting the food on the two plates they had. Pastor then led them to the place of honor at the center of the head table.We then found a place in line, filled our plates, and proceeded to find a place at one of the tables to sit. When we were almost done eating, the Master of Ceremonies got up and announced that the ladies would begin serving the wedding cake. He then asked the pastor to say a few words. This was followed by several congregation members making some comments. It was at this time that Fred was asked if he wanted to say a few words. Fred stood up to speak.

He stood at the table looking around the room for what seemed to be several minutes not saying anything, just looking. A hush fell over the room. The ladies began serving the wedding cake. He then looked down lovingly at Ella, took her hand in his, bent down, and kissed her lovingly on the forehead. She looked up at him and gave him a warm smile and wiped a tear from her face with a paper napkin.He looked again at the assembled congregation, cleared his throat, and with emotion began to speak,

"Ella and I thank you for this wonderful surprise and this wonderful meal. We suspected something was up when some of our friends began acting strange when the subject of our anniversary came up. The pastor really let the cat out of the bag when he announced this at the beginning of the service today. This really is more than we ever dreamed of, and we thank you all for this wonderful meal."

Again, Fred stopped talking and looked around as though he was using the pause to compose himself. He began to speak again.

"As most of you know, Ella and I grew up in different parts of the state. We met purely by accident. It was after the war, and I was with friends in the big city. She was in the city looking for work."

His demeanor became more serious as he continued his story.

"What you don't know, and I have told Ella this many times. That I knew Ella long before we ever met. We have been blessed with 60 years of life together plus a couple of years together when we were dating, but I knew Ella for a long time before that, we just hadn't been introduced yet."

"In my heart I knew Ella. This goes back to when I was in my youth and decided that I would read the Holy Bible cover to cover. It so happened that around that time, I was attending confirmation class at the Lutheran church where I grew up. Put that together with the fact that I was just finding an interest in girls and you have a confluence of intellect, emotion, and desire."

"From the Bible, I learned about love and responsibility, that this was the foundation for marriage. In my confirmation class, I learned about sin, judgment, and salvation. From my human nature, I experienced the attraction, the companionship, and the desire for a girl. Girls were all around me, but in my heart, I knew only Ella. The question then became which of the multitude of girls was Ella?"

"Our Lord works in wondrous ways. I was a teenager absorbing everything around me and I was reading the King James Version of the Bible. I was very systematic in my Bible reading. For my confirmation class, I was looking up those verses listed in The Lutheran Catechism and following the lessons the pastor was presenting."

"It was at night when my school homework was done that, I would open my Bible and read. I started in the beginning with Genesis and was reading through it book by book, chapter by chapter, and verse by verse. When I came to Chapter 31 verse 10 in the book of Proverbs, I found the answer and met Ella!"

"Verse 10 asks the big question of finding the woman that was dear to my heart. From the verses that follow I drew up an outline of who Ella is. She is trustworthy, loyal, faithful, industrious, diligent worker, good manager of the household, compassionate, of good reputation, praiseworthy, and God-fearing."

"I believe that God planted the image of Ella in my heart and that our accidental meeting was his plan. I continually thank The Lord for my Ella and for making us a part of His plan."

At this point he leaned down and kissed Ella on the cheek. He stood up again and concluded.

"Again, Ella and I thank you for this afternoon." at this, he sat down.

The Master of Ceremonies stood up and said a few words. The pastor stood up and said a few words, and the crowd began to leave for home. I went home with my friend and his family and after we talked for a while, I left for my motel room. I still think about what Fred said, I think in some aspects he may be right. Maybe, just maybe I knew my wife before I met her.

Encounter

George is returning to Atlanta from a week of sales calls in Florida. He is driving alone heading north on I-75, a little way past Ocala. The 1976 VW silver Scciroco is humming along nicely, the CB radio is squawking the usual static, and the radar detector is on in readiness for any signal that might be sent his way. The sales trip began Sunday afternoon with an eight-hour shot to Jacksonville. Now, it is Friday, and George is heading home. He should get there in due time, that is if the *sleepies* don't get him first. Even the pressure of eighty miles an hour and the constant fear of *"Smokies"* (State Troopers) isn't keeping him awake.

Here is the first Gainesville exit and George enters the expressway off ramp to buy *"motion lotion"* or gas for the car and a caffeinated drink for the driver. The gas is $6.00, and the Coke is $.40.

"What else can he do to stave off the sleepies," he wonders as he leaves the gas station to get back on the expressway.

There at the side of the onramp, stands a man with a sign which reads Michigan. How many times has the wife been upset with him for picking up hitchhikers? Too many times to count. But, there is fatigue. As he enters the ramp, George looks at the sign and the lone person standing there holding it,

"He looks harmless enough," he thought.

He is about six feet tall, very thin; he was wearing blue jeans, white cotton t-shirt, oxford shoes with no socks, and no bulges from his pants pockets. He looks safe enough, and George stops to pick him up.

In the ten years that George has been traveling, he has developed a way of relating to hitchhikers, just a few rules to keep him out of trouble: First, have nothing visible that will give away your name and address where he can get at it. Second, be vague about your background. Thirdly, have a glass coke bottle within easy reach to use to bean the guy with in case he gets *"strange"*.

George stops the car a little past where the hitchhiker is standing, reaches across the passenger seat, unlocks the passenger door, and pushes it open.

The hitchhiker picks up a small canvas bag and hurries toward the open door.

"Put the bag and the sign in the back seat over by my briefcase, and welcome aboard," George instructs the hiker,

"You can call me Joe."

"Thanks!" replies the hiker, "You can call me Harry."

"Where are you headed?" George asks.

"Lansing Michigan," comes the reply, "and you?"

"I live in the Atlanta area," George responds, "I can only give you a ride that far."

George, his wife, and their six children have lived in Atlanta seven years now. They had been married in 1963 when each graduated from college. He had taken the corporate route in marketing with a large company. She hadn't taken a job and was the perfect wife and mother.

Over the years, the company had moved them here and there. They had lived in the desert and by the seashore, but now they were living in Atlanta and she had plans to never move again no matter how many job opportunities had to be passed up. The more George looks at Harry and hears him speak, the more familiar Harry seems to be. The person he reminds him of was more heavily built, but the face, and the mannerisms seem so familiar.

Harry sits silently for a while listening as George talks to the truckers on the CB radio exchanging positions of the last seen "Smokies" and such.

Finally, he speaks,

"Where in the North did you come from? You sure don't sound like the typical southerner!"

"Wisconsin," George responded not wanting to give out more information than that.

"Me too, after high school, I joined the Marines and saw the world, but I ended up in Michigan," Harry responds.

That last statement was it. George knows where the voice comes from. This person sitting beside him in the car sounds like the Harry he grew up with back in his little hometown in Wisconsin. Yet, something has changed the man next to him. He seems but a shadow of the friend he once knew.

"Where did you start from?" George asks.

"Some place you would have never heard of," is the answer.

A long moment passes.

"Ever hear of Albion?" Harry asks.

"Sure, when I worked in Wisconsin, I used to stop at the Allis Chalmers Tractor Dealer there and buy gas. The dealer is on Highway 51 right across from the Creamery. Sure, I remember Albion!" George replies.

George has a hard time keeping his voice in control because he was in shock. Sitting beside him in his car going, 70 miles an hour appears to be his old friend, from his youth, Harry. George could understand how it was that Harry wouldn't recognize him. After all, he hasn't seen him in about twenty years, and during that time he has changed a lot. He now wears a full beard. He is at least 100 pounds heavier now.

He has survived an accident which had changed his facial features somewhat. That is why he wears the beard, to cover the scarring. After the accident, the new false teeth he got have changed the shape of his lower face. All his friends had commented about this at that time. It is no wonder Harry couldn't recognize him.

George reaches down to turn up the volume on the CB radio. Listening to what will help keep his mind off of what he just learned, until he comes to terms with it.

"Joe; that is your name isn't it? When do you think we will arrive in Atlanta?" Harry asks.

George thinks for a minute and answers,

"If we can keep up the speed, we will be at the I-285 junction in about six hours. If not, it could be eight. It just depends on the 'Smokies'."George met Harry in the boy scouts. George lived out in the country in an old house, surrounded by farmland. His parents rented it because it was cheap.

Harry lived in an old house on a knoll in Albion with a farm at the back of the house and the village somewhat to the front.

George lived with his parents in a stable family; not rich, not poor, but definitely comfortable. Harry lived with his old maid aunt. George remembered when Harry's father deserted him and his mother. He also remembered when his mother went away, came back, and then went away again.

Their backgrounds were so different, yet somehow, they were attracted to each other. They liked to get together and *fly* their model airplanes. Airplanes with engines, that ran on a special fuel developing enough power to keep the little planes airborne. The control for the planes was from two wires coming out from one of the wings.

The wires were about fifteen feet long with a handle which controlled the altitude of the plane. They stood holding the handle and the plane flew around them in a circle. The trick to flying them was to not become dizzy as you turned in circle to control the plane as it flew around you.They learned to play chess together upstairs in George's room in front of the gabled window which looked out over the little woods at the back of the house. They worked together to become tenderfoot, and to rise up the scout ladder. They shared their fondest dreams and their deepest fears with each other.

Then one summer day Harry was gone. The village was buzzing with the gossip of how Harry's mom had returned the night before in a big car. Some said it was a Cadillac, some said it was a Buick. She had come to retrieve her son. They recounted the argument they thought they heard, on that clear night, coming down to the village from that farmhouse on the little knoll.

They told of the mother making fun of the simple life in the country and describing the excitement and glamour she could finally share with Harry in the *City*. They said Harry's aunt made accusations of the mother being a loose and fallen woman who would only lead Harry to ruin. Some claimed they saw the silhouette of Harry and his aunt hugging before he was led, some say, crying into the car. Others claimed to have heard the faint sounds of crying coming from the house on the knoll far into the night.

Several men *who know*, spoke of Harry's mother coming into Andy's Bar and Grill down by the river on the other side of the village before she went to get her son. No, they didn't see her car, but she now had blonde hair, wore a low cut tight black dress, black high heeled shoes, and a fur piece made to look like foxes, one holding on to the tail of the other, going around her neck. Yes, she did have a drink. Yup, it was one shot of whiskey straight. Time passed slowly and not much happens in little towns.

George was in high school now. It was the dawning of the age of Elvis. The hair styles were changing in the small farming areas. George's dad had even been able to buy the two-year old big Buick four-door sedan he was learning to drive. Things were going well at scouting, he finally made Eagle.

Other things were also going well for George. There was this sweet young girl who sat the next row over from him in Science class. She was tall, thin, had black hair that hung down with curls, an impish smile, and deep blue eyes. She seemed to like him, and he liked her. He even had a song he sang to himself woven around her name, Karen. Karen, a name that brought a warm feeling to him.

They were in few classes together, as she was considered a *city kid*, having gone through eighth grade in the school building across the street from the high school. The *city kids* were considered in a different social class than those bused in from the country school system. Because of this quirk, they were only together in the classes such as Science and Math, although they were also in voluntary activities such as Drama Club.

If there was a romance, it had only progressed to hand holding and gazing into the eyes, but things progressed much slower in the small towns back in those days. It was a Tuesday morning, when George, on his way to gym class, passed the principal's office. It was a normal curiosity which caused him to look through the door into that office every time he passed it and this day was no different. This time though he was in for a shock, for there in the principal's office stood Harry and his aunt.

George finally located Harry during the lunch hour and went slowly up to him to say hi. The weather was discussed, the time was noted, and they promised to meet after classes and go to the soda shop for a soda before the bus came to take them home.

In Science class, George whispered to Karen and passed her a note about Harry. In the note he told her he would not be able to keep her company as she waited for her bus after school as he was going to get a soda with Harry. She indicated in an answering note, she signed with X's for kisses that she understood. As it so happened before she could successfully pass that one on to George it was intercepted by Mr. Brewer the teacher.

Mr. Brewer, probably to discourage note passing, looked at the note and reckoned as he didn't know who the note was for; and that he didn't wish to stand in the way of true love as with all the X marks for kisses along the bottom of the note, he guessed he would have to read the note to the class so as to be sure that the message was delivered.

As he read the note Karen blushed and put her head down in her arms on the surface of the classroom desk chair. George kind of slouched down in his desk chair trying not to be seen. When the bell rang to end the class, George wanted desperately to talk to Karen, but Mr. Brewer cornered her as she was about to leave delaying her longer than George could wait and he had to leave for his next class.

George was preoccupied through the next classes with the aching that goes with wanting to talk to Karen, but not being able to make the connection. The final bell rang, and school was over. George first found Harry and then took him to where Karen was waiting for her bus. He hadn't planned to do this, but after that embarrassment in class, he really had to talk to her before the day ended.There, he introduced Harry to Karen as his old friend from Scouts. George and Karen talked for a minute, then her bus came and she was gone without her and Harry even having had a chance to talk. George and Harry walked to the soda shop and each claimed a stool at the counter. Together, at the same time, each in an independent action, ordered a Vanilla Phosphate soda. They were under the impression that the vanilla was preserved with a little alcohol which made this a really *cool* drink. It was at that point George knew Harry was back.

Over the next few months, Harry and George were like twins. They generally could be counted on to do the same things. If Harry wore a red shirt and blue jeans, it was a sure bet that George would get off the bus wearing the same combination. When winter came, and last year's coats were dusted off and worn to school, they even had the same style of coat.

They were in Drama Club together, Stage Crew together, Debate together, and even both signed up for archery. Harry lived near enough to a farm that he could join FFA, however, George not really living on a farm, but out in the country joined Library Club. Karen was usually seen in the same activities that the two guys chose except she was in Library Club.

There were also other differences though. Harry came back to school a year ahead of George as he had been advanced an extra grade when he was attending school in the city. Although he was a grade ahead of Karen and George, he was actually some months younger than both of them. He had learned a special sophistication during his years in the city which came across in his wit and self confidence.

Things began to change between George and Karen, too. They no longer stood by the side of the pillars at the front door of the school holding hands and gazing into each other's eyes as they talked. Now, with Harry always there, the holding hands and gazing seemed awkward. They still held hands as they walked, but they didn't have the alone time they had been used to.

At first, George wanted very much for Harry and Karen to like each other. Later, he didn't know if that had been such a good idea. He felt Harry's sophistication and fast talk were slowly taking Karen from him.

Winter turned into spring and the time for the Drama Club spring play was upon them. George had a part; it was not the lead, but he played a substantial character that was killed off in the first act. This was necessary as George was needed to direct the stage crew for the intricate scene changes which came in the second and third acts.

Harry had a small part and was in charge of the lighting. Karen was assisting the director and was also in charge of the makeup. The last few weeks before the play was performed, involved many evening rehearsals. By this time, George had his driver's license and was bringing to and taking home half the cast from the evening rehearsals.

He tried to work it so that he could take Karen home last, so she could sit next to him as they rode around dropping off the rest of the kids, and this gave him some alone time with her in the car when she was dropped off last. Unfortunately, this meant going almost home to drop off Harry and then back to the other side of town for Karen.

After his father had commented about the excessive miles appearing on the Buick each night, George had to compromise and drop Karen off early in his route. The best way that worked out was for her to ride in the back seat with Harry.

Needless to say, the play was a success.

The next big affair that spring was the Junior Prom. It was open to anyone in the school and was the social highlight of the year. George really wanted to take Karen to the Prom, yet he didn't know where to get the money. The whole night would cost a minimum $100 and that money just wasn't there. He should have seen this coming and planned for it, but he hadn't.

Harry had asked several girls, but each had refused. He talked to George and seeing that George was not going, asked if it would be alright for him to ask Karen. George didn't like the idea one bit, but friendship was friendship, and it is awfully hard to turn down a friend. Harry took Karen to the prom.

After the prom, things were never quite the same between George and Karen. The three were still seen everywhere together, the hand holding was less frequent, and then seemed to disappear altogether. The talking and gazing didn't happen anymore either. The school year ended soon after. Harry graduated and the summer vacation was there.

George's father had managed the local paper for all those years and would probably still be in that little town, but a friend in a large city needed someone to run one of the departments at the paper he worked for. The money offered was too much to turn down, so by the end of June, George and Harry were saying their goodbyes.

Before school ended for the year, George being able to use the car, and since both of them were juniors, Karen's mother allowed them to go out on dates. George had been very happy about this and tried his best to win her, but the gazing was gone, and her goodnight kisses were more sisterly than romantic.

When the moving truck was loaded and they drove away from the only house he had ever known, there on the front lawn waving goodbye were Karen and Harry holding hands.

George often wrote to Karen, but after a while her letters stopped coming. Later that year, he heard through some friends that Harry had enlisted in the Marines and Karen had become pregnant. The next time Harry came home, he and Karen were married.

George continues checking on the CB radio and driving fast to make time, but he is having a hard time thinking of what to say to this long-lost friend. Should he fess up and welcome Harry in a manner that long lost friends do? Or should he keep his emotional distance and not let Harry know his secret? This is the inner turmoil going on in George's mind. He had gone away to school, met his wife, and was happily married. Yet, he still felt the hurt from losing Karen. Harry had been his best friend and yet...Harry keeps looking at this Joe fellow as he drives, as though he recognizes so many things about his voice and the way he speaks that do not go with the face. George keeps remembering back to when he was growing up and yet not all those memories are pleasant, especially those about Karen. They are now north of Valdosta and the caffeinated drinks he drank earlier are heavy on his bladder. He needs to stop and asks Harry if he needs to do the same.

They stop at Adel where George tops off the gas tank and they both take the *necessary rest*. When they get out of the car, George makes sure to lock the car before leaving it. He tells Harry that this is to make sure nothing is taken when they are in the store, but it is also so that Harry has no chance to find out who Joe really is.

They both get something to drink. George gets a coke, Harry gets water. George makes it a point to notice if Harry has some money with him. He does, but it doesn't look like much. George pulls back onto the expressway and again gets on the CB radio.

This is around the time in the day that channel 19 is rather quiet and he gets no comebacks. He slows down to a little above 60 miles per hour and relaxes a little in his seat. Five miles an hour over the limit should keep him out of trouble.

He looks over at Harry and asks him what had brought him to Florida anyway.

Harry looks over at him and replies,

"I was at the Veterans Hospital in Tampa to have something looked at, old war wounds."

"That's right; you said you were a Marine," Joe acknowledges.

"Were you wounded in Nam?"

"Yeah, in Nam."

There followed a long silence during which Harry just sat there and hung his head.

"You call Lansing home then, or are you just going there to visit?" George asks.

"I really don't have a permanent place to stay. I just have friends and old wounds in Lansing. I have reasons to go back there though. Mostly, I stay around the Tampa area. The weather is better, and I can pick up some work now and then," comes his somewhat depressed reply.

"I guess you don't have any family back in Wisconsin then," probes George.

"I had an aunt, but I let her and a bunch of other people from there down when I left. I went back to visit for a while..."

As he spoke his voice broke and his thought hung in the silent air in the car only interrupted occasionally by the crackling of the CB radio.

Again, there is that void brought about by neither man being able to speak. George is pondering what he is hearing and trying to get answers to questions that have haunted him since he had left that small town. Yet there sits Harry, his onetime best friend, the one who had eventually won the heart of his first love, Harry who has all the answers to his nagging questions, and he has yet to find a way to ask them.

The CB is virtually silent with no traffic, so George adjusts the squelch to lessen the static, adjusts the sensitivity on his radar detector and holds his speed. He has been having a hard time concentrating on the traffic since all this is on his mind. He really doesn't need a speeding ticket on top of this.

Harry is sitting quietly on his side of the car nervously and endlessly folding his hands together as though he were washing them.

"You said you worked around Tampa. What kind of work do you do?" Joe asks.

"Just odd jobs, yard work, swimming pools, and things like that when I can."

George thinks about that answer for a while and then asks,

"Does your business have a name?"

"I know some guys who need help now and then, I work for them, and they pay me cash. That is the easiest," Harry painfully answers.

"What is your address? I might be able to touch base with you the next time I'm in Tampa?"

George is trying to find out more about Harry and thinks this might be a way.

"I live with friends and at the hospital. I have problems sometimes," Harry evasively states as he crouches deeper into his seat.

"I'm better now, that's why I am going back to Lansing. I might be able to stay there at least for a few months."

George thinks for a moment and comments,

"Those must be some pretty good friends to invite you to come and live with them for such a long time, friends from Nam?"

The road noise and the crackling coming over the CB are the only sounds in the car as Harry weighs that question for some time. Finally, he turns to George and says,

"I have a daughter in Lansing. Her husband works in a plant there. I am going to try to find work there."

George doesn't answer right away. He calls out on the CB for a front door but gets no response. The radio is quiet except for the static. He lets a little time pass and asks,

"You have a wife in Lansing then?"

"No, that ended a long time ago. We were married young and had a daughter before I was posted to Nam. It didn't last. It was during my second tour in Nam when we were divorced. She now lives in Wisconsin. We haven't been in touch for years. After the divorce, I wasn't as careful and that didn't end too well. I kept in contact for a while and there was child support. I still tried to be a father to my daughter. That was not easy after I was wounded."

They are a little south of Macon, so George gets back on the CB radio to see what the bypass is like. There is some chatter so he adjusts the squelch to see if he can hear more, but it is still too garbled to make anything out.

George breaks the silence between them with another question,

"How old is your daughter?"

George thinks he can keep him talking which accomplishes two things, one, it makes the trip seem shorter, and two, he seems calmer when he is talking. George thinks he has hit on a pleasant subject because Harry seems to perk up a bit as he begins to talk about his daughter.

"She just turned twenty. She went to secretary school and while she was there, she met this young man from Detroit. They dated about a year when they decided to get married. When he graduated from the classes he was taking; he got this job in Lansing and they live there now. I couldn't afford to go to the wedding, but they came to Tampa during their honeymoon. I met him and we hit it off. He invited me to come to Lansing to find work. He thinks he has found something I can do. He even met with my doctors at the hospital and talked with them about it."

"That sounds pretty good. I hope it works out well for you," George replies.

Now, the wall has been broken down and Harry begins to talk about his past. He was a Marine and he is proud of having been in the service. He had been wounded and had almost died. He doesn't talk about his wounds or where he served, he was just doing his duty.

He talks about a girl named Karen and how she and his best friend George had been so close. How George had moved away, and Karen and he had become so close. How he so loved his daughter and doted on her when he came home on leaves. How over the years, long-range love slowly went away until finally he lost Karen.

Then Harry looks at George and says,

"Joe, if I close my eyes, I think I am sitting next to my old high school friend, George. Then I look at you and you look nothing like him except for your eyes. I swear you have his eyes. Joe, it's like somewhere out there you have a twin and his name is George."

George fiddles with the CB radio with his head down so Harry can't see the moisture in his eyes. Harry closes his eyes and rests on his side of the car. They don't speak for quite a while. George is torn inside, but it is for the best that Harry never knows who he really is sitting beside.

They are past Macon and on I-75 passing to the east side of the Atlanta Airport when Joe asks,

"Where will be the best place for you to get your next ride?"

"I don't know," Harry replies.

"Lansing is still at least two days hiking from here. Do you have money to spend the two nights in motels?" George asks.

"I'll be alright. I can sleep under a bridge or something."

"Do you have a warm coat or even a blanket inside your canvas bag?" George enquires.

"I'll be all right," Harry reassures him.

George makes up his mind and drives into Atlanta to the bus station.

"I never had to go to Nam, and I have always honored those who served there. Can I buy you a bus ticket to Lansing? That way you will be warm and be able to sleep on the bus and get there a day earlier."

Harry doesn't answer; he just reaches into the back seat and retrieves his sign and bag. George goes in and buys Harry the one-way ticket and pays for it on his credit card. He says his goodbye, gets in his car and begins his drive home.

As he drives, he thinks of ways to explain to his wife what he had just done. He had just spent money from their tight budget to send Harry to Lansing. And he knew he would have to then suffer her scolding for picking up the hitch hiker on his way home.

The Father's Son

Monday mornings are becoming earlier and earlier again, and this one began at 4:30 a.m. On the days that I fly, most of this was because of the fact that an early flight means being early in the office to do those last-minute Monday morning things such as last-minute notes to the secretary, pick up my tickets and boarding pass, etc. Then there is that dash through forty miles of traffic to the airport.

This Monday morning, all I could think of was to get to that airplane, board at first call to take my favorite seat which was two rows from the back on the aisle, snuggle up with an airplane blanket plus pillow, and make up for lost sleep. That might not sound like much of a goal for a Monday morning when you are supposed to spring out of bed, run to the mirror, tell yourself you are the best, and arrive at the office ready to take on the world. Well, on those early Monday mornings that I fly, I am ready to take on the world as soon as I wake up at my destination.

I arrived at the airport, checked my bag, checked my flight number in the display but found no gate listing. There was a concourse, but no gate. I then proceeded to the concourse listed and went to the display at that location to find the gate number for my flight. I joined a group of distinguished-looking men all with their eyes looking towards the display.

I addressed the group in general and asked in a loud voice, "Anyone going to Jacksonville?"

I knew I was standing with the right group of distinguished-looking men when most of them laughed. I started a conversation with one of them. He was a salesman, naturally, and he also was a frequent flyer. We passed the time of day as salesmen (read those distinguished-looking men) generally do, selling to each other.

Finally, a boarding gate appeared. *Fantastic!* We, the distinguished-looking men moved, like a herd of thirsty cattle heading towards a watering tank after a barrier had been removed. We went towards the assigned boarding gate. The flight was posted to leave on time, but that would be in twenty-five minutes; and we all wanted to leave on time.

I had been pretty cool up until now. I had kept my sleepy attitude and was still ready to board, curl up, and sleep. The first thing that got my adrenaline up was the stampede from the display to the boarding gate. I read the flight number and destination. The flight posted to leave this gate was not my flight number and the destination was Birmingham. Having lead the stampede, and if you go fast they won't trample you and most of them being older, get winded early in the stampede anyway. So, I was first to notice this. Now, this really woke me up.

As we milled about in front of the counter at the gate, an agent made the announcement that due to equipment failure, the Birmingham flight had been cancelled and the passengers were being re-booked on a later flight. About thirty grumbling passengers were ushered from the gate. When they were finally safely away, the agent changed the Birmingham sign and numbers to those for Jacksonville, FL.

We, the milling throng, heading for Jacksonville, had been given this nice plane.

It seems that it was our plane that had suffered the equipment failure. I guess this was a case of sacrificing the cost of flying a few in this plane, for the profit of flying *"the many"* to another destination. In any case, the posted departure time was now only ten minutes later than our original scheduled time. The gods of *on-time-service* must be appeased. We were hurriedly advised of our new seat assignments and the rush to board was begun.

Now, my new seat assignment was 20E. This is not my kind of seat. Being a larger person, I find it difficult for me and uncomfortable for my row mates if I sit next to a window. I discussed this with the agent and was told the flight was overbooked because of the equipment change to the smaller plane and I was lucky to have gotten any seat. I asked about first class since it was relatively empty.

Well, I, followed by several others of the stampeded distinguished men, made a quick decision. We, as frequent flyers, could upgrade opening more couch seats for the rest of the passengers. I now had seat 2D, still a window seat, but a view with room in the seat, in first class. Maybe, just maybe I could get my nap now.

Fate or whatever you call it, a course of events which sometimes works to waylay your best plans, struck again to deprive me of my much sought after sleep. As I was getting nicely settled into my seat for the next hour's nap, who to my *wondering eyes* should appear, but the person assigned to seat 2C. He placed his briefcase under the seat ahead of his and backed himself into his seat.

I could have ignored the decal on the side of the briefcase. I could have turned my head the other way and closed my eyes, but now I got that adrenaline shot one gets from curiosity. Wasn't that emblem the same as my old school alma-mater? I was sure! It was upside down and slightly out of the focal distance for my glasses, but it sure looked like it was. Now, at last I was undone, no sleep until I find out.

We began to talk. He seemed much younger than me. He was from my old hometown and that sure was the updated version of our college emblem. We talked about business and work.

His name was Frank and he was an Electrical Engineer who did troubleshooting all over the country for his firm. We discussed my product and he mentioned that his firm used my product in their equipment and purchased it through their northern office.

We began to reminisce about the old neighborhood and the large company that had been its lifeblood. We marveled that such a large manufacturing facility had now been turned into a shopping center of all things. And the memories came flooding back.

I told him how I got my first job at that now defunct company in the summer of 1959. He told me that he hadn't been born until 1960. I told him of the fun I had getting to work in my old car and the problems we had in finding parking places. He told me of how his dad had worked at that old company and had walked to work in those days because they lived so close.

I told him how I had grown up on a farm and was relatively new to city life at that time. He told me how his father had emigrated from some Baltic country as an eighteen-year old man and had begun working in the machine shop at that now defunct company in 1948.

"The machine shop?" I asked.

"The machine shop," He replied.

"Once a year, our whole family would tour that place and see the machine he used to operate."

I found out that his father had been there, probably running a milling machine during the same time I had been there running a drill press. I described his father to him. He said he remembered the old pictures of the man I described. What cinched it was when I described his father's accent.

We were still comparing notes when the plane landed. I never did find out what his father is doing in retirement because we had to get about the business at hand, deplaning.

The gods of *on-time-service* were appeased as we arrived only five minutes late. I never did get that nap, but I left that plane marveling at the coincidence which placed the son of a man I had known thirty years ago in a seat next to me and had allowed us to find our connection.

In parting, I gave him my business card to give to his father. I wonder if his father will even remember me, as I was a short-timer there and being young, never said much. He gave me his last name, Janeck. I wished him and his father well and he waved as he headed for his ride.

So much for my early Monday morning nap but missing that sleep didn't bother me all day. As I went about my business, I remembered back to those long gone days in a long gone machine shop eating lunch in a circle with a group of men, noting a somewhat shy man with an accent, who although part of our group, said very little. Those warm memories kept me awake.

The Right Seat in the Car

It started sometime after my wife died. It happens at night, it is just there. It feels comforting and it is strange. It happens in the right seat of my car as I drive to my next town at night to work in my territory.

I have been a traveling salesman for most of my working life. I currently cover most of the five states, but in the past, I have covered as many as seventeen. My work is such that I am away many times on weekends. I drive my territory, so my trips take me away from home for as many as three weeks at a time.

It was my habit to always check in with my wife at around 9:00 p.m. each evening to pick up the messages from my home office phone. This way, I could follow up on them the next day. I always printed a detailed copy of my schedule so that she could contact me and leave *important* messages at the motel that I would be staying at that night.

There were some days when she had other places to be during the evenings that I would be on the road. She would add notes about these on my schedule, and with that, I would know that I need to call her early the next morning. This system worked well for us as she always knew where I would be, and she had the freedom to do the things that she was interested in when I was away.

We never thought to make provisions for contacting me if some emergency should come up on nights when she was scheduled to be at home, or for some other reason of not being able to take my 9:00 p.m. phone call.

Despite my constant travel, we remained emotionally close. And many nights, we would talk for hours on the phone sharing the little things that had happened to each of us that day. Sometimes, we would talk of things we wished we could have done together that day and at times, would talk of what we hoped to do when the day would come when I could afford to retire and remain at home.

There was a time when she tried to ride with me on some of my trips, but there was nothing she could do except wait in the car while I worked with my customer, and that was no fun for her. It was also more expensive for her to come and that made some trips a losing proposition.

Our kids have all grown up and were out of the house so to speak. They were scattered all around the state, but the closest one was in a little town about twenty miles away, and we would talk to him occasionally. We would try to get together and do some family thing once a year. We were young enough, so the kids were not in the habit of checking up on us regularly as some do with their parents.

I was on the second week of a three-week trip, about 250 miles from home, when it happened. The report indicated that it was dark that January night, and it was surmised that she had made a trip to the local grocery store. Apparently, she was trying to rush home to be there for my 9:00 p. m. phone call. She was about four miles from home at an intersection of two roads controlled with a four way stop sign. Approaching the intersection from her left, was this drunken fellow in a raised four-wheel-drive truck with big tires approaching the intersection at a high rate of speed.

He lost control of the truck as he entered the intersection and his right front wheel drove right over the left side of her car, at the driver's door, crushing it. The bottom of the truck snagged the car and the momentum took both vehicles into the ditch where they came to rest. It took some time to get a wrecker to the scene and to be able to remove her body from her wrecked car.

That night I got to my motel late, so I planned to call her before I went to eat my supper. I called as soon as I had reached my room and I only got my answering machine. I unpacked and freshened up a bit and called again with the same result. I double-checked my travel schedule to make sure I hadn't missed any notes that she might have added to my schedule, and I found none.

I turned on the TV and waited for another fifteen or twenty minutes and called again, still the answering machine answered. This was unusual for her not to be there or to at least not listen to the answering machine. I became very nervous and began to worry. But I tried to calm myself.

"Something must have come up", I reasoned in my mind.

I went out to get some fast food to bring back to my room. I found the McDonalds which had a drive through open this late at night, and I bought something to eat. Back in the room, I tried to call again. I still got the answering machine. And now, I was really worried.I called my son to see if he knew anything. He hadn't heard from his mother, but that was not unusual. Next, I called the neighbor across the street. She looked across the street and reported that the house was dark, but the garage door was still open. This was strange as my wife never left that open when she was at home, and she usually closes it when she left for any length of time.

The neighbor volunteered to go across the street and check on the house. I agreed that it would be a good idea and I would call her back in fifteen minutes to see what she had found. I quickly ate my McDonalds meal and called my neighbor back. She had gone over to the house and found the house locked up and dark.

She walked around the house and pounded on the front, back, and the garage entrance doors with no result. Together, we decided that this was very strange for my wife to be gone like this. I thanked her for her help. Now, I was bordering on frantic and I am sure I was running on adrenaline. What to do?Next, I called my son again. When he answered, he knew something was wrong just from the sound of my voice. I told him his mother wasn't answering the phone and I was concerned. I told him about the neighbor and what she had found. He, too, became concerned, and we decided that he would go to the house and as he had a key and would go inside to see what he could find.

He was very reassuring that this might be a false alarm and there would be some perfectly logical explanation. He told me to calm down as he would find out what the problem was and call me back in an hour. I was instructed to wait in my room, get some sleep, and wait for his call. I tried to nap which didn't work. I watched some TV to try to kill time, and waited nervously for his call.

It was an hour and a half before he called me back. Now, he sounded concerned. He reported that he went through the house and found nothing, locked up the house again, and closed the garage door. He had found no sign of his mother. He told me he had made a phone call to the city police department and reported her missing and asked that they keep a look out for her car. It was after midnight and I couldn't sleep, so I explained to him that because this was so unusual and I was worried, I would check out of my room and begin my drive home. I guessed I should be home by 6:00 a. m. and I hoped by that time his mother would be at home.

On my drive home, many scenarios of what could have happened to her went through my mind. Could she have gone for a ride and had been carjacked? Obviously, she hadn't expected to be gone long or she would have closed the garage door.

Could her car have broken down and she was stranded someplace where she could not get help? I should have bought her a new car last time. New resolve, I will not hand down my company car to her when it is time to change vehicles no matter how good of a shape it is.

Could she have become ill and was stranded along the side of some road waiting for help? But she is in good shape. She is so young yet. New resolve, she should go to her doctor for a complete physical check-up and soon.My desire to get home to her along with my massive adrenaline surge kept me on the very edge of my seat and my foot heavy on the accelerator all the way home. Sleep was nowhere in my mind. I was sharp as a tack and irritating the heck out of the speed limit. I arrived at the house around 5:30 a. m., hit the garage door opener and parked in the garage. It seemed strangely empty without her car parked there beside mine. I went into the house and literally collapsed on to the nearest kitchen chair. Where could she be?

I called my son to let him know I had made it home safely. He mentioned that he had heard nothing back from the local police department and felt that was a good sign. He still sounded very worried and volunteered to take the day off from work and come over to the house so that we could go about looking for her together. I thanked him for his offer, but I didn't think that was necessary, and told him that I would check around with some of her friends to see what they knew and said good bye.

While I was gathering my thoughts, I, out of pure mechanical reaction to the stress of the situation, began to make breakfast. I sat for a while just looking at my cereal and toast and then decided that I must put my day together. I had begun to become sleepy and realized that I had been up for at least twenty-four hours, and I would have to get some sleep. Then I remembered where I was supposed to be this morning. I went out to the car and got my briefcase and got on the phone cancelling the calls for the rest of the week.

I sat down in a family room chair to plan my next move to find my wife but I fell asleep. It was about 9:00 a. m., when a loud knock on the front door of the house woke me up. It persisted long enough for me to wake up from my drugged nap to get myself out of my chair and answer the door.

Standing on my front porch was a sheriff's deputy. He introduced himself and began asking me questions. He asked my name and if I lived there. He asked if my wife lived there and I answered yes. He asked if my wife was missing, and I answered yes, and that she wasn't at home last night and her car wasn't in the garage this morning when I got home.

I was still groggy from my lack of sleep and I was not answering his questions very well. I could see the confusion on his face, and I began to explain.

"I am a traveling salesman, I called home last night to pick up my messages and talk to my wife, but she was not home. I called my son and he called the town police and I drove all night to get home. I suppose you are following up on my son's call," I told him.

He looked at me and asked if he could come inside. I invited him in and then he told me to sit down. He chose a chair across from mine and joined me.

"Last night," he began, "at about 8:15 there was an accident at the ... Crossroads."

"It was a bad accident," he said, and he was sorry to inform me that my wife had been killed.

"Her body was taken to the county morgue." He said I could make the arrangements with a funeral home and her body would be released as soon as it was convenient. In answer to my questions, he gave me more details about the accident, but in my state of mind, at the moment, I remembered few of them.

I called my son and the other kids and put in motion what was necessary for the funeral. By that afternoon, all the kids with their family had come to the house and each helped, each in their own way, as much as they could.

Together, the kids and I made the funeral arrangements. She was so mangled in the crash that we could not view the body, so we chose to have a closed casket. We scheduled the funeral home visitation for the evening before the funeral. She would be buried in her family's burial plot in the local cemetery.

My wife had many friends that I had never met. I was surprised how many people came to the funeral. So many people gave me condolences and stated how she would be missed. By this time, I was numb. It was heartening that she had so many friends and that she had had such a full life when I was gone, but nothing could fill the emptiness I felt and the feeling of loss of the things we had planned that would now never happen.

One by one, the kids and their families all left, and I was all alone in the big house we had shared. The good memories were there all around me, and yet the loneliness and emptiness that pervaded the house was almost overpowering. The second week after the funeral, I turned my focus to my territory and began to call my customers to set up my next trips, but I was not yet ready to travel.

I had to get out of the house, so I visited the wrecked car in the wrecker company's storage yard. The driver's door and the top had been crushed into the front seat that it had to be cut away to get her crushed body out. The yard was open to the elements, but there had not been enough dew or rain to wash the blood stains from the driver's seat upholstery yet.

It was parked near the wrecked truck that had so mangled it. I went and visited the crash site. It looked peaceful and undisturbed. It was interesting to see how nature had already covered up the scar that had been a place of death.

Next, I took care of all the legal things necessary to make sure that the drunk driver would be properly prosecuted for the accident. I used the time I took off from traveling to reorganize my house and to adjust to being alone. I had been traveling alone so much that I reasoned that it wouldn't be that hard living alone, but I was wrong. The longer I stayed home, the lonelier I became, and that brought on depression.I soon found a secretarial service and made the necessary secretarial arrangements, so I could get back on the road. I rearranged my life around my work schedule and reasoned that if I worked hard enough and long enough, I wouldn't have time for my loneliness. I now redoubled my focus on how I worked my territory.

I developed a new routine; coming home only long enough to do laundry and what paperwork I needed for my work. And yet, loneliness was my biggest problem, the one I just couldn't seem to conquer. I missed her so much. I am not one who ever believed in ghosts or the supernatural. I say this because I still don't believe what is happening.

And this is how it happened:

After I had slipped into a rather routine travel schedule, I noticed unusual things happening in the right seat of my car. I had returned to my usual routine of working the day with the salesman in one city, and after concluding my business with him, I drive in the evening and sometimes at night to the next city on my schedule. During these drives, that begin at about sunset, I began to feel like there was a warmth emanating from the right seat of the car. It was as though something was comforting me. I would move my hand over to the seat and could not really feel any difference, but the perception would not go away. I checked the heating and air conditioning system in the car and played with the vent adjustments to no avail. Finally, I decided that I was imagining things and tried to ignore the feeling.

A little time passed, but the warm feeling hadn't gone away as I drove to my next city, and something else began to happen. Usually, I got to my next motel before it was very dark, but as the days got longer and Day Light Saving Time came into play, I began working later with my sales people, which meant that it became later in the day when my trip to the next city began and I was more often driving into the night.

At times, I would feel the warmth more intently and it was as though my peripheral vision, I saw a shape occupying the car seat beside me. This was not distinct, it really had no form, it seemed like it was just there. I would turn my head and look only to see nothing. *What was happening to me*? I began to try to rationalize this away. It wasn't happening. I was just seeing things that weren't there. *Was this happening because I was a lonely old man? Or was I exhausted and just needed sleep?* Then I noticed when I was driving along, other things seemed to happen. I would look to the side and start to change lanes, and it was as though for a moment the steering wheel wouldn't respond. I would look again, and there beside me would be a car that I hadn't notice. That momentary stop of my action had avoided an accident. These things were happening frequently, and I began to worry that I was beginning to lose my driving skills. I began to concentrate more on driving safer.

Finally, one dark night, driving along on my way to my next motel, I began to talk to the shape I was seeing in my peripheral vision in the seat next to me. I do this regularly now. I address the illusion in the name of my wife and somehow it relieves me of my loneliness and the warm feeling comes over me; I think I have a passenger.

Note: this story is dedicated to the Salesman I worked with who's wife died suddenly while he was away at work in his territory.

The Social Circle Affair

It was 2:15 a.m. September 21, and I had just checked in at checkpoint number three, Social Circle, on my nightly Augusta to Atlanta run. I was a driver for the We Be Gone Messenger Service. The night was dark, there was no moon, but clear with a multitude of stars visible. The little Ford was perking along at 55 miles per hour, the most efficient speed and the batteries showed three-quarters charge, I had finally learned to restrict my fluid intake and my bladder wasn't even uncomfortable.

And then it appeared. I first noticed two headlights in the rearview mirror. Had they been bright like the modern LED's, I probably wouldn't have noticed, but they were kind of a dull reddish yellow. The second thing I noticed was they were gaining on me faster than they should, even for a speeding car. At this time of the night, there were seldom any vehicles on this expressway, so I drove in the smoother left-hand lane. I had the car in automatic-drive-lock, which meant the Ford followed the road automatically at the proper speed even if I fell asleep. I could, if I wanted, override the system and drive up to ten percent faster or slower, but I couldn't drive as fast as he was going, as he seemed to be rapidly gaining on me.

I slipped the leaver out of automatic-drive-lock into lane-change and the car picked up the proper road signal and automatically began the lane change while I watched the lights continue to gain on me. I wondered how this car could be traveling at such speed and how it could get this close without the proximity program in the road slowing it down.

Just as my car finished its lane change and the automatic-drive-lock leaver switched from lane-change back into automatic-drive-lock, the vehicle attached to those strange lights passed me as though my car, going 55 miles per hour, were parked. That car must have been going 90 or better when it passed me, I thought. I watched that thing speed on ahead of me in the left lane until the red taillights vanished in the distance.

As the Ford continued moving in the right lane, I sat in my seat and shook. Never in my computer-controlled driving had I experienced such a close brush with an accident in my life. All the cars since 2025 had onboard GPS assisted computer navigation systems. These systems were guided by reading magnetic signals buried in the surface of the highway and GPS assistance keeping the vehicle at a safe preset speed on the desired expressways until the vehicle reached the programmed destination.

The program was specifically prepared to prevent another vehicle from coming closer than what was considered a safe distance on the expressway. There hadn't been a freeway accident in at least fifteen years. Was I losing confidence in the system? I had never been this close to an accident. This was my first, I was shocked. How could this have happened?

I was too busy shaking to get a good look at the car that passed me. The vehicle was fast, the night so dark, the speed was so great that it just seemed like a blur in my mind. After all, this was a new job for me, my first big driving job. Just think, I am driving five days a week. One round trip per night. This was my second week on this route, and the last thing I needed was an accident.

I finished the trip without any further incidents, turned my cargo in at the warehouse, parked the car, and went home.

The next night when I checked in to work, there was a note taped to my locker door instructing me to see the dispatcher. The more I thought about the incident the night before, the more dreamlike the memory became. Reason dictated that in this age it must have been a dream as it just couldn't have happened. By the time I picked up the note and headed for the dispatcher's office, I had pretty well convinced myself the situation never happened. I think that's why the dispatcher's words were such a shock.

The dispatcher asked me about how the car was running. He had never done that before, but maybe they did that every two weeks, or so I thought. I answered that I thought it ran well and gave me no trouble, everything had worked fine. He explained that the car recorder which recorded the whole trip every night had a problem.

Every night, the computer did a fast scan to determine the mechanical condition of the car and how the car performed each day. This prevented on the road breakdowns which years ago had cost the company millions of dollars in lost business. I told him I understood the program and the car had run fine. He then asked me what had happened at 2:15 last night.

When I asked why, he answered that at that time, when I passed Social Circle, there were five minutes of blank time recorded in the computer memory. That for five minutes, the computer marked time but nothing about the trip had been recorded, then after the five-minute period everything that happened was again recorded as though nothing had interrupted the input of data.

He turned to me and in a fatherly way asked,

"Tell me what happened, son."

I told him about how this strange car that had come up behind me so fast and passed me, literally almost forcing me off the road and causing an accident. I explained how I had changed lanes in the nick of time to avoid the accident.

The dispatcher was silent for a while as he appeared in deep thought. It was eerie just watching him. He looked as if he was trying to weigh each word, he was about to say something to me. But he just shook his head and motioned me to leave.

I left his office and went to the assignment board, picked up my trip info, and headed for the assigned Ford car. It was a different one than the one I had yesterday, and the battery charge showed about 90%. I went to the charging station for a quick charge so I could be sure to make the round trip without a fuel stop in Atlanta. That night, I ran late and passed the Social Circle check point at approximately 3:30 a.m. The trip went smooth and I didn't have a car ahead of me or behind me all night.

Due to having a quick charge on this Ford every night, I was running a little late for the next four weeks. Other than that, everything was going so great that I pretty much forgot about my almost accident.

Then it was October 19, and I had a newer Ford which allowed me to depart right at the scheduled tine. I was driving along in the left lane as usual with the Ford on automatic-drive-lock having just checked in with checkpoint number three, Social Circle, when I looked at the time. It was right at 2:15 a.m. I got this funny feeling in the pit of my stomach, and immediately changed lanes.

It was not a moment too soon. The Ford had just settled back into automatic-drive-lock, when in the rearview mirror I saw the strange eerie lights in the distance gaining on me. Now, I had time and decided I would give that car a once overlook as it passed me. I wanted to see what kind of car could travel that fast on this computer-controlled highway.

I looked in the mirror to try to see the shape of the front of the vehicle. Looking into the glare of those lights made it impossible, even with the modern specially treated glass of the mirror.

It caught up with me and passed. It was almost a blur as it went by, but I was able to determine two things: first, the body style of the vehicle reminded me of something I had seen in an old car museum, and second, the wheels seemed to be making sparks as they rolled on the highway.

I don't know how to really explain the sparks. The closest would be to those brief spark showers we see when we watch the debris re-entry in the sky after a night launch of a Delta Airlines sub-orbital shuttle, or the sparks one sees when one rapidly drags a piece of raw steel across a concrete surface and it *sparks*.

Well, those wheels continued to throw sparks as the car sped away at this high rate of speed. As the car passed me, I had enough time to read the license tag and get a number. This was an old-style Georgia tag such as collectors now display. The number stamped into the metal was SOX-905 and the date seemed to be 1976. On the rear of the car above and to the right of the license tag, I read some chrome colored letters which appeared to read DASH--. One thing was for sure, whoever was driving west on the expressway was driving an illegal vehicle with an expired tag.

I finished the rest of this leg of the trip to the Atlanta terminal with no other unusual things happening. My return to Augusta took place without incident. On my drive back, I placed the Ford into automatic-drive-lock and relaxed. As the car continued, I began to assess the facts of the situation. I now knew the license tag. The design of the car was unusual, but I had part of its name, DASH--.

The year on the tag was 1976, sixty-five years ago. Maybe that information could be traced. After much thought, I decided that I must come up with a plan to find out more about this person who apparently seems to be bringing an illegal car onto the expressway. Up until now I had felt that the law banning all cars not computer operated from the streets and roads was silly.

I had heard and read about the great numbers of people who had died on the highways before computers controlled the speed, distance, and destination of the car, but the close call to an early death sobered me and made me agree with others that these old cars were dangerous and must be banned.

By the time I arrived back at the Augusta terminal, I had made up my mind on the course of action for the next night. I had finished my run with no trouble. I left a note for the dispatcher telling him I would be in early the next night to talk with him. And when I got home, I slept like a baby.

The dispatcher was looking for me when I arrived at the terminal. I could tell by the look on his face that he probably had already received the report on the computer readout from the car. He seemed nervous as we walked to his office. Once inside, he shut the door and motioned to a chair. I sat as he sat at his desk across from me.

"You want to talk about it?" he asked in a demeaning tone.

His accusatory attitude set me off. I asked in a demeaning voice, "Why don't you tell me?"

"How long have you been working here?" he demanded in return.

Something wasn't right here.

"Could I talk with the last driver who had been making my run?" I shot back.

I must have hit on a problem as he then asked,

"Have you been discussing this with any other employees of We Be Gone Messenger Service?"

I could see that we would continue to ask questions back and forth for some time with neither of us giving any information to the other. This reinforced my suspicion that the WBGMS Company had something to hide and was not telling me all I should know. I quickly decided to change the direction this was going.

"I guess you got the computer report back from the mechanics," I stated in a matter of fact voice.

"How did you do it?" he demanded.

"I didn't," I answered.

"What time are you due out?" he asked.

"In an hour," I replied.

"Do you object to having security in here with us when we discuss this further?" was his next question.

"Why would he be necessary?" I asked.

"He is necessary if you want to keep your job," he replied.

"You hired me, I can get another job," I replied.

"When we get through with you, you will be in jail and never drive again!" he threatened.

This began to sound serious and it appeared that I didn't have any more cards to play, yet the only thing I had done was avoid an accident with an illegal antique car.

"I called this meeting. I didn't realize I had to bring a lawyer," I stated.

"You realize by tampering with the computer recording the trip you broke a federal law," was his answer.

With that the door opened and two armed police entered, and I found myself under arrest with my hands cuffed together being led away. Fortunately, I was able to post bond, but I knew I would have to see an attorney the next day and this little episode began to look like it might be more than just my job. Here, I was innocent of any crime and yet how could I prove it.

I went home and for the first time in about six weeks, went to bed by 2:00 a.m. At least I was going to get a good night's sleep and around 10:00 a.m. be in a good mood to search for a lawyer. I even had the names of several in mind. And with good thoughts like those I went to sleep.

It must have been 3:30 a.m., the exact time is sketchy because of the circumstances, when the police burst into my bedroom waking me. I was immediately handcuffed and hauled away in my underwear to be booked again. I wasn't even read the charge, but I got the feeling it had to do with smuggling, robbery, or something like that.

Naturally, I was upset, no, livid. I vowed I would sue. I yelled and complained, but the night court where I have been taken earlier was not in session any longer, and I was placed nearly naked, cold, and shivering into a holding cell with about twenty drunks. I did get some sleep, but not much before I was pulled from the cell to be taken before a judge for arraignment.

I was still shivering in my underwear when my turn came before the judge. I didn't understand the charges against me, but this time I objected vigorously to the judge. I said it was unreasonable to connect me with whatever happened because I had just returned from Night

Court and went to bed – there wasn't any time for me to have done anything.

The judge checked the records and found the facts and although the charges still stood, I was released in my own custody.

It was nearly noon when the police cruiser dropped me off at my home. It was really my final bit of stubbornness that got me the ride home. I wouldn't leave court in my underwear and I had no clothes. I complained that I had no money either as that would have been with my clothes. The judge decreed that the arresting officers lend me a uniform, not a jumpsuit to go home in. It was the judge's opinion that they should have given me time to dress before bringing me here and to take me home in a jumpsuit would unnecessarily embarrass me in front of my neighbors. The final compromise was me wearing a long coat belonging to an officer and the arresting officer driving me home.

When the officer left with the coat, I picked up the telephone and called one of the lawyers on the list I had put together in my head early this morning before I went to sleep. His secretary answered the phone, took down my name and address, and I waited. Eventually, the lawyer came to the phone and when he heard a little of my story explained that he could not possibly have the time to take my case.

He did say that he had a young and able junior member of the firm who could handle my case and this person would see me as soon as I was able to come to the office. I dressed and immediately headed for his office.

I entered the office and approached the desk of the person I thought was the receptionist. I introduced myself and waited for her to summon the person to take my case. I expected to see a smart young man in a suit and tie come through the door and announce that he was going to represent me.

Instead, this young-looking woman sitting behind the desk stood up facing me. Here in front of me stood this thin young woman, approximately five feet two inches tall, blond hair, blue eyes, and wearing slacks who announced that she was going to represent me.

She ushered me into a conference room and motioned for me to sit at the table. She picked up an iPad and sat across from me.

"Explain the situation to me." she instructed.

I explained about my job and answered her questions concerning the details of what I knew I had been charged with. After about an hour of going over the facts as I knew them, she went to a computer to review my arrest record and the charges against me. She reviewed the copies of the court records she had obtained from the computer with me.

As we read through the charges, it became more and more obvious what was happening to me. We sat together and came up with a strategy to try to settle this matter before it went any further and got much worse. It was now late in the day, but she was able to contact the lawyers for We Be Gone Messenger Service and make a date to meet with them at the WBGMS office the next day at 3:00 p.m.

When we arrived at the WBGMS offices at 3:00 p.m., we were ushered into a conference room and told to remain there. A security guard had already been stationed there, apparently, to guard us, as though we were a threat. We were told to sit in some chairs. We waited and at about 3:15, the others arrived. The head of security entered first, followed by the lawyer, the dispatcher, the supervisor, and an armed police officer.

After exchanging formal pleasantries, their lawyer and my lawyer settled down facing each other across the large conference table in the center of the conference room. When I began to follow their lead and position myself beside my lawyer, they motioned me away. After some time, I was allowed to join them. I sat next to my lawyer and they all sat across from us at the other side of the table.

Their lawyer began to speak,

"We lawyers have agreed to get this session underway in the most judicious way. To do this we will bring the known facts of this situation to light."

"Fact one, approximately two months ago, a bonded employee of WBGMS apparently found a way to escape from the moving courier vehicle and disappear into the night with whatever it was that he was stealing. He accomplished this fete without us knowing how he did this by causing the recorder to malfunction for about five minutes."

"After five minutes, the recorder began to again record. The question is how he manipulated the digital record to advance for the required time and yet record nothing in essence. Then leave a blank record and then begin to record as though this had never taken place?"

"Fact two, the gap in the record was studied, but nothing could be determined from it. Although, when it was timed against another recorder, it indicated the vehicle must have maintained an average speed of 55 miles per hour to have reached the place on the highway where it began again to record."

"Fact three, our suspect drove two different vehicles yet on two occasions he was able to affect each vehicles recorder, so that it did not record for a period of five minutes. Oddly enough, the five-minute intervals were always in the same place on the highway."

"Fact four, our suspect was able to accomplish this fete on two different vehicles."

"Fact five, the driver of the vehicle who made the run night before last, one of our most trusted men, a supervisor, didn't complete his run. He checked in at checkpoint number three, Social Circle, and was never heard from again. The vehicle arrived driverless at the Atlanta terminal."

"Fact six, the record from the vehicle was analyzed and had a five-minute dead spot in it occurring at exactly the same spot as the three previously mentioned."

"Fact seven, there have been no recorded losses of any consigned property or anything else which was supposed to be delivered as contracted."

"Fact eight, in light of this conspiracy, last night's run was cancelled costing WBGMS to have to lose a considerable amount of revenue."

"Conclusion, there has been a conspiracy to smuggle some substance between the two cities and that the night before last night's messenger was the innocent victim of this conspiracy and may be dead.

It is further concluded that the accused is a part of that conspiracy and may be an accessory to the murder of the last driver."

After hearing the charges read, I felt a little disgusted to think that I had been accused of this *crime*. I also felt scared that I would be convicted of something I had no knowledge of. I conferred with my lawyer assuring her that there was no truth in any of the things I was accused of. She assured me that this was probably a power play of some kind to shield something funny that the company was doing, and she had something in mind.

My lawyer took to the floor and working from notes on her iPad, described the experiences I had related to her about the illegal antique car. She even gave the information about the license tag; the tag number was SOX-905 and the year 1976.

What she said next was a complete surprise to me. It was a stroke of genius on her part.

"My client feels very strongly about this illegal vehicle which almost ran him off the road and has concluded from what has been said that this vehicle may be involved with whatever illegal activity is taking place. Therefore, my client is willing to work with the law enforcement officers to catch this vehicle. To this end he wants to drive the Augusta-Atlanta run tonight with the head of security as a rider and with an appropriate state police car near as a chase vehicle," my lawyer offered.

The participants on the other side of the table got up from their chairs, went to a corner of the room and formed a huddle from which whispering, and coughing could be heard. They remained in this huddle for some time. Eventually, the lawyer and the head of security along with the police officer returned to the table. They informed my lawyer and me that my offer had been accepted with one addition. The speed governor on the Ford would be disconnected in case things became violent and we would have to speed away.

My lawyer accepted this with no reservations.

That night the Chief of Security and I got comfortable in the Ford and began our drive. The Chief had a two-way radio which was tuned to the police frequencies. As we drove, he talked back and forth with his police contact. The state patrol would intercept us about ten miles east of Social Circle and drive with us to Atlanta with the prime interest being that six mile stretch of road west of Social Circle. I drove as I had on the other occasions so as to reach the critical checkpoint number three just before 2:15 p.m., I timed it so we could slow up a little if we had to await for the arrival of the illegal car.

All went well; we were joined by the State Patrol cruiser at the agreed point. There were two State Troopers in the cruiser, so we felt doubly safe. The cruiser took up the pace driving in the left lane on manual and we were in the right lane driving in automatic-drive-lock. The two vehicles were driving side by side. The chief of security was reviewing strategy with them when I gave my report at checkpoint number three.

I watched the time. I was fifteen seconds ahead of my schedule and 2:15 showed on the time display. I looked in the mirror and got a sinking feeling in the pit of my stomach as saw nothing there.

"Had it stopped happening?" I asked myself.

Apprehensively I looked in the mirror again, nothing.

Then suddenly, in the distance, I saw the faint glow of the funny reddish yellow lights. This was reported to the State Troopers who made a quick decision to hold our position. The strategy was to box the car in and not let it pass, then slowly reduce our speed. This would force the car to slow down to the point where they could make an arrest. I watched the lights gaining on us. The car wasn't slowing down; it just kept coming.It got closer and closer, but showed no signs of slowing down. The troopers were on the radio indicating that they were expecting to take a hit and this would eventually slow the car. Our instructions were to hold position and accelerate out of the way at the last minute. We watched horrified as the car continued to gain with no sign of slowing down a bit. As the car came close to impact, the trooper on the radio kept saying,

"Hold your position, hold your position; hold your position!"

Now I was driving the Ford in manual override as I watched in the side mirror as the antique car began to make contact with the police car. I had to be very careful not to veer from the right-hand lane into the left lane and bump the police car.

The chief of Security was sitting sideways in his seat belt in the seat beside me holding the hand-held radio and watching to the back as the old car seemed to make impact.

Then they touched, but there was no sudden sound of impact. I watched, the chief watched, and what we saw couldn't have happened. It was impossible and I still don't believe what I saw. The old car kept coming right through the State Patrol vehicle as though it didn't exist. The headlights first penetrated the trunk; then were seen in the back seat, then the inside of the car lit up as though there had been an explosion and the headlights continued until they were shining out the front of the car. The entire old car passed through the state vehicle.

After the light from the seeming explosion died away, the front seat of the State Patrol car appeared to be empty. When the old car passed through the state vehicle, it appeared to have totally removed the occupants in an explosive ball of fire. Within seconds, I had to veer to my right and accelerate as fast as I could to avoid the driverless car. I watched in horror as the State car lost speed, fell behind, and in less than a minute destroyed itself in a ball of fire, and then there was alarge explosion in the median strip of the expressway.

The whole time, the Chief of Security tried in vain to raise a response from the State Troopers, but the airways were quiet. No response came except for a comment from the base where they had been monitoring the situation.

The Chief instructed me to step on the accelerator and try to catch that old car. I tried to comply. I was draining the batteries at a dreadful rate. I was traveling at over 100 miles per hour when I finally caught up and was beside the car. This was definitely an old car, no doubt about it. As the Ford drove even with that old car, I saw shapes in the seats, but it was the driver that I was watching.

He appeared gaunt and drawn with a deathly smile, but what sent fear into my heart and trembling into my bones were his eyes. I have never seen anything similar nor have any of my friends reported that they have ever seen anything that could describe that looked like this. Here looking over at me had to be the very face of death. The Chief of Security gasped and stopped trying to raise the State Patrol base on his communicator. We were out of range. He sat there silently as we continued along beside this phantom car.

Then, as we reached mile marker 100 on the expressway, just as suddenly as it seemed to appear behind us, it began to vanish beside us. First the front disappeared as if the front was cut off from the rest of the car. As the car continued forward the rest disappeared the same way. By the time we had passed the 100-mile marker, the whole car was gone. I immediately slowed the car and placed it in automatic-drive-lock. I looked at the battery indicator and hoped we had enough charge to make it to the Atlanta terminal. Just to be safe, I dropped the speed down to 45.5 miles per hour to get us there with a little charge to spare. As soon as the Ford stabilized, the Chief and I looked at each other. He was shaking so hard he couldn't hold the communicator. I was also shaking so hard my teeth were chattering.

As soon as he was able, the Chief tried to raise one of the close police cruisers on his hand-held radio to make sure that the State Patrol Base knew about the accident. He got no response. Although I knew I was out of range, I still tried to raise checkpoint number three on my radio, but there was no response came from there either. The Chief concluded that we could do nothing for the burned-out wrecked state vehicle, so we should continue our run to the Atlanta terminal. He took it upon himself to note this in the Ford trip computer.

When we arrived at the Atlanta terminal, I took care of the routine business while the Chief went into the office and phoned the State Patrol to give his preliminary verbal report. The battery in the Ford was so depleted that it couldn't be quickly charged in time for us to return to Augusta. I was able to find a replacement but that took a while. Our return trip had to wait for that, but once we started, the return trip went well although it was way behind schedule. We slowed at about the 100-mile mark to gape at what was happening in the median where the Patrol car had crashed and burned.

We returned to the Augusta terminal to a quiet welcome. There, we met with several officers from the State Patrol, the President of We Be Gone Messenger Service, their lawyer and my lawyer.

The President took my lawyer and me aside and made small talk with us while the Chief of Security, their lawyer, and the men from the State Patrol talked on the other side of the room. I was tired from the drive and all the excitement, so I didn't pay much attention to what was happening. I stood there amidst all the activity and tuned it all out.

After about twenty minutes, the dispatcher, the supervisor, and the company lawyer ushered us into that room from which we had plotted our strategy eleven hours ago. Only this time we didn't sit at opposite sides of the table, we kind of all sat around it. The company lawyer began by reading all the information he had read from the first meeting adding, "Fact nine, the computer readout of the Ford for tonight's run showed again a five-minute gap,"

My lawyer took the floor and added some new data she had uncovered:

"Fact one, the rouge car was a 1974 Volkswagen Dasher two door coupe."

"Fact two, the license tag reading was SOX-905 licensed in 1976."

"Fact three, the car was owned and driven by an Industrial Diamond Salesman."

"Fact four, July 21, 1976 this car crashed and burned killing the driver."

"Fact five, the investigation found that the car had been traveling at a high speed at the time of the crash."

"Fact six, according to the microfilm archives from the State Highway Department, the body was burned beyond recognition and the car was a total wreck. Later, it was taken to a junk yard."

The Chief of Security then gave his detailed statement as to what had happened. And I gave my report.

My lawyer again took the floor. She asked that under the circumstances, all charges against me should be dropped, that her fee be paid by the company and that I be compensated for my trouble. The company lawyer agreed to all her requests and assured me that my job would continue with the company.

The representative from the State Highway Department stood up and made several very interesting remarks. First, was that the disappearance of the several drivers and the two troopers obviously was caused when their vehicles were overtaken by the phantom car traveling in the fast lane of the expressway.

Second, that it was to my credit that I saw what was behind me and reacted fast enough to get out of the way the first time I saw the car.

Third, that this being the sixty-fifth anniversary year of the original accident, this phenomenon had to be either a time warp on this section of the expressway, or was one of those rare occurrences mentioned in history as an apparition or a full blown poltergeist.

Fourthly, that he was in no position to argue what it was either way, but from now on until something else can be arranged, all traffic would be delayed at that time of the night so no vehicle would be in the area at 2:15 a.m.. So that this kind of loss of life would never happen again.

The President of WBGSE stood up and told us how important to the safety of the area that this be kept a secret. It would not due to have all kinds of thrill seekers on the expressway looking to see this thing in the middle of the night. Imagine how many would end up getting hurt. And we were all sworn to secrecy.

Two months later, I arrived at checkpoint number three a little early and was able to talk the State Patrolman into letting me enter the zone early. I promised him I would be out of the zone before the phantom car came through, but I lied. I wanted to see the phenomenon one more time. I drove slower than usual and sure enough there it came speeding up behind me.

I looked at the car as it drove by and could see the driver clearly. I don't know if it was real or my imagination, but I swear that when that car passed by, there were two state troopers and two drivers all packed into that little car with that wild eyed driver.

I still don't believe it, but I swear I saw it. The two State Troopers in the back seat turned and waved to me through the back window as the car pulled away. The next morning, I went in early and talked to the dispatcher and no problems ever came from that indiscretion.

That was many years ago. That old stretch of superhighway no longer exists. Eventually, that stretch of that expressway was rerouted to the north. I often wonder though, if I were to go out in those old fields at 2:15 p.m. would I be able to see that old car coming across the field one more time?

North Little Rock Motel

Dear Pastor Bob,

During our discussion about spirits last night, I remembered a situation I experienced back in the early 1980s. I decided to write the experience down and send it to you.

I was then selling Capital Equipment through a string of distributors throughout the south. The type of equipment has no bearing on the story, except the best way to train the distributor salesmen to *sell in my absence* was to take a product demonstration literally *on the road*. I called this my *"Dog and Pony Show"*.

On this occasion, I had planned a rather rigorous schedule to cover in two weeks what had usually been covered in three.

It was a Monday. I had driven for seven hours and kept a 1:00 p.m. appointment with one of my Memphis, Tennessee distributors. After having a successful meeting, I went to my second Memphis distributor to hold a 6:00 p.m. on the same materials.

I really should mention that in my younger days, I frequently held three sales meetings a day. Usually, these were 8:00 a.m., 1:00 p.m., and 6:00 p.m., after which I would drive for four hours to the next town to repeat the exercise. Usually, I ended up averaging four hours of sleep a night. You know, younger fellows can put up with those kinds of schedules.

In any case, I left Memphis late to drive halfway across Arkansas on I-40 to my motel reservation in North Little Rock. This had been a long day. I was more tired than I thought, which meant I had to stop frequently to buy the caffeine laden Coke-A-Cola that I drink to stay awake on the way. I arrived at my motel late, safe, and full of Coke. I checked in, was given my room key, parked at the back of the motel, and proceeded to the elevator with my luggage. The room number was 319, a corner room, third floor, *outside*, right around the corner from the elevator.

"This was very convenient," I thought, *"At least I don't have to drag my suitcase real far this late at night."*

I entered my room and began getting comfortable. I adjusted the temperature to make the room nice and warm. I always sleep better in a warm room. With nothing on TV that late, this was before the advent of cable, I just relaxed on my bed. And with that much Coke in me, sleep eluded me.

I believe it was nearly 2:30 a.m. when sleep finally came. I definitely remember psyching myself up for the sleep I needed. I had a meeting in Little Rock in the morning, and two in Fort Smith, one in the afternoon, and the other in the evening. As far as I can remember, the next night was to be spent in Tulsa.

Being as my body was full of Coke, I knew I would be up to go to the bathroom about once an hour, so I prepared accordingly. You probably do the same thing when in a strange motel room. Before I laid down to relax, and not have to get up again before sleep overcame me, I cleared a path. This would be the one I would have to take, so I could make it to the bathroom for relief without stumbling, banging around, or otherwise cause damage to myself.

To further enhance getting there, I turned on the bathroom light and closed the bathroom door. I remember doing this as the light coming through the crack at the bottom of the bathroom door was easily seen reflected in the full-length mirror on the wall at the foot of my bed. I gazed at it wondering if it would keep me awake, but it didn't as I eventually went to sleep.

I awoke at about 3:30 a.m., and surprisingly, I didn't wake up because I had to pee. I woke up because the room had become very cold. I was under my covers and yet I was freezing; I woke up because of the cold. And since I was already awake, I decided to relieve myself. The room was dark, so I felt my way around the foot of the bed and found my way to the open bathroom door and went in and turned on the light. I finished what I was doing, turned to leave and instinctively closed the door.

Then it hit me, I was sure that earlier I had turned on the bathroom light and closed the door. Well, it was late at night and at that point I didn't care how come the door was open and the light was off. The room was still so cold. I went over to the wall unit to set the temperature so it wouldn't get cold again. *"Didn't I set up the heat when I went to bed? I'm sure I did, but I was tired and must have forgotten."* I thought, but I was exhausted, and sleep came quickly.

It was around 4:30 a.m. when I woke up again, shivering to a clammy chilled room. As I lay there under the covers wondering why I was so cold again and why my covers hadn't kept me warm, I decided to take one more trip to relieve myself just to make sure and to turn up the heat again. I looked out from under the covers to a very dark room. There was no bathroom light, and from what I could see in the shadows, the bathroom door was open.

"What's going on here?" I thought to myself.

Now I remembered.

The first time this had happened, I thought, *"Al, it's late, maybe you turned the light off somehow and just didn't remember, and the room just got cold. Forget it and go to sleep. Now, this is the second time it happened the same way as the first. This couldn't have been an accident. Something happened here."*

After doing my duty, switching on the bathroom light, and closing the bathroom door as before, I spent the rest of my night sitting in the bed. My back against the pillows, propped up against the headboard, watching in the mirror that crack of light coming from the crack at the bottom of the bathroom door. If this were going to happen again, I was going to see it.

Later that morning, about 5:30, as I was checking out of the motel, I asked the desk clerk if anyone had reported any strange occurrences' in the motel lately.

She looked at me, then at my room number on the key and with a knowing smile replied, "You got caught in the elevator, didn't you?"

I didn't answer.

"We are going to have to do something about that elevator. The elevator people are trying their best, but ever since that man died of a heart attack in the elevator six months ago, the buttons just seem to get pushed. Would you believe, the elevator has been known to continue going up and down, with people trapped inside, for as long as twenty minutes? Some nights, it will go up and down for hours. With your room so close I suppose it kept you up all night," she explained.

She must have seen the shock on my face because she called the manager over and said, "He didn't sleep very well last night, he was by the elevator."

Before the manager had a chance to use the canned speech, he probably had prepared and ready for this specific situation, I asked him if he had had any trouble with lights and the air conditioner being turned off in room 319 in the middle of the night.

After I explained the events of the early morning to him, the motel manager took me aside and began to explain. It seems many years ago that that wing of the motel was built over an old Negro cemetery. The developers knew when they bought the land, but they didn't tell anybody, although when the plans were revealed, and the blacks in the area protested, there was nothing legal they could do.

When this was built, there was not yet the equality of the races that there is now, and the State Historical Society didn't care about preserving or moving one Negro cemetery located on prime development land. He indicated that the strange things happening at night in that wing were not unheard of and that is all he would say.

I continued the trip without any further incidents. In my travels through that area of Arkansas, I have always avoided staying at that motel.

Lost Baggage

I am sitting here at this airport computer terminal and entering my story, which you are reading on your monitors. I am doing this only to try to make sense out of this. I know that you are reading this because I am disrupting the flight information which you normally use these computer monitors to find. I see all of you trying to find a way to make this computer system of yours react to your inputs in a normal manner. I assure you that I will be through writing in a very short time; however, until then all you can do is watch and read. All I want is an answer. An answer to the question – what or where am I?

I completed my sales calls, turned in my rental car, and made it to the Tampa International Airport early. I stood in line at the ticket counter and when my turn in line came, I asked the agent if I could get my ticket changed from the 3:14 p.m. flight to the one at 1:30 p.m. The agent was cordial and very happy to make this change.

As she began that simple task, she looked at the monitor and asked,

"Would you rather leave on Flight number 257, which will leave at 12:50 p.m. instead? There is still time for you to make it to that plane."

"Yes," I answered.

All was in order; I had my ticket, boarding pass, and baggage claim check. I headed for the shuttle car that would take me to concourse B Gate 27. Naturally, I proceeded to the gate in haste. I try to get there in plenty of time to board and become comfortable in my seat. I used to fly 100,000 miles a year on an assortment of airlines and airplanes, and nothing that was done was in any way out of the ordinary. My seat was 34D, an aisle seat and the man sitting next to me was friendly. What more could be asked?

The plane I was on was supposed to have left the gate at 12:35 p.m. on 17th of January. Due to some unforeseen difficulties, it was delayed to 12:50 p.m. which was why I was able to get a seat, checking in as late as I had. Leaving late, however, caused concern to some of the riders as they had to reach Atlanta in time to make connections with other airlines. The captain assured all of us that this would be no problem.

The takeoff took place without difficulty and the stewardess appeared with the beverage snack right on schedule. I looked out the window at a light blue sky over fluffy cotton-like clouds which hid the land beneath from my view. We flew at an altitude where there was no turbulence. The whining of the engines finally worked their usual magic on me, so after the stewardess picked up the remains of the snack, I began to doze.

I usually don't sleep through landings, but when I awoke the plane was at the gate. I don't know what it was that awakened me, but I looked around the plane and all the seats were empty. This was unusual, and no stewardess had awakened me to check my seat belt and straighten my seat back for landing. We were already at the gate.

Apparently, the man in the seat next to me was able to get up from his seat and climb over me to deplane without awakening me. I unbuckled my seat belt, arose from my seat, stretched, and retrieved my briefcase from under the seat and my hat from the overhead bins.

I walked down the aisle to deplane. And as I left the plane, the captain, who was talking with the stewardess, wished me,

"Goodbye, have a safe afternoon."

As I was walking up the ramp away from the plane, I checked my watch. It read 2:10 p.m.

"*We made good time,*" I said to myself.

When I reached the concourse, I noted that I was at gate B-34 and had a long walk to the people mover area of the airport to catch the train to the baggage claim area. An airline employee at the next gate, with the task of routing the incoming passengers who must change planes to the proper gate, asked me if I needed any help. I told him that I didn't and proceeded to the airport people mover.

The concourse was rather crowded, and several people would have run me down if I hadn't used very evasive action. It was as though they didn't see me. I made my way down the escalator to the people mover trains and waited. There were several other businessmen waiting for the train. We discussed how crowded the concourse had been for this early Friday afternoon.

The train came and I got on for the ride to the end of the line. I took the escalator up to the baggage claim area. I looked at the screen of the viewing monitor which listed the arriving flights and the carousels on which the baggage for those flights could be found.

I read the flight numbers, but my flight was not listed. I stood looking at the monitor and waited. After flight number 257 had not yet appeared on the monitor screen and twenty minutes had passed, I became restless and began to look around. I could recognize no one from my flight waiting there with me. I, and I alone, from flight number 257 was left waiting for my baggage.

I thought to myself, *"Where could everyone be?"*

I decided that in the half-asleep daze I had been in ever since I had awakened in the airplane at the gate; that I must have arrived at the baggage area too late to claim my bag. Many times when most of the bags were claimed they would shut down the carousel and take the remaining bags to a holding area.

I walked back and forth in front of the unclaimed baggage holding area looking for my bag and found nothing. I finally went to the lost baggage claim area, opened the door, and went in. I placed my briefcase near the door and stepped to the rear of the line to await my turn at the desk.

The people in front of me were making claims about the usual types of lost luggage, one suitcase out of three, a small handbag, or a flight bag. I then finally got to the front of the line. I asked the

Stories Told by Traveling Salesmen

overworked girl at the desk about luggage for Flight number 257. She phoned to some place.

She told me that there had been some equipment problems with one of the automatic conveyor belts and that the baggage should be up in in half an hour. With that, she dismissed me and asked to help the next person in line.

I picked up my briefcase and left. I still hadn't seen anyone I recognized from the flight waiting around for their luggage. This must have been an unusual flight to have had everyone except me either connect with another flight or have carried-on all their luggage.

I waited by the monitor, it would take half an hour to fix the baggage problem, for my flight number to appear.

"What can I do? I must go home pretty soon." I kept thinking. As there was still no number on the monitor screen.

I returned to the lost baggage claim area. I had been on the ground, by my reckoning, for at least one and a half hour and was becoming tired and a little out of sorts. In desperation, I cornered an airline baggage agent in the lost baggage area office and demanded that something be done about my luggage from Flight number 257. She went to the phone and called out to some area, baggage operations I think, and turned to me really upset.

"What is the meaning of this? Is this some kind of sick joke? If you don't leave here I will call the police. No, stay right where you are while I call the police!" she said, sounding very disgusted.

"What do you mean? Here is my paperwork for the flight, and my claim check!" I answered, which only seemed to cause her to become more upset.

"What kind of a creep are you?" she demanded. "That flight, as you very well know, crashed on its approach to the airport and burned at about 2:00 p.m. this afternoon, anyone coming around here asking for luggage from that flight has to be sick!"

That information didn't sit well with me. I thought she must be kidding. I handed her my ticket, boarding pass, and baggage claim check. She read them over and fainted dead away falling like a rock to the floor. I reached down for my briefcase which I had set on the floor beside me when we had first begun to talk. But I couldn't find it; it had disappeared.

Suddenly, I didn't feel so good. I noticed people around me trying to awaken the agent on the floor. I bent over to try to help wake the agent up and it seemed as if people were stepping through me. More and more people arrived in the room and one walked right through me.

"Where am I? If anyone knows, answer me on the screen." I released the computer.

Addendum: *The setting for this is the early 1980s when air travel was much freer with fewer restrictions.*

Magic Forest

You commented about the hole you saw in the wall when you looked through the door into the upstairs bedroom. Let me tell you a little story.Ten years ago, my wife and I moved our family into this new neighborhood. Part of the beauty of our new home was its setting. Here, was this beautiful English Tudor house nestled among the majestic spreading Live Oak trees. Interspersed among the oaks were some dogwood and evergreen trees. The name for the subdivision really set the tone for its beauty, *Magic Forest*.

The sign at the entrance read, *Magic Forest; Four-bedroom homes built on five acre lots in an enchanted setting*, that was how the original sign was worded. Soon after we bought the house, that sign was removed and replaced by a smaller one lettered in Old English Script simply stating *Magic Forest*.

The new house we bought had a magical charm. Once inside, the twenty-first century world seemed to give way to a world of dreams and fantasy. The children fell into this routine rather well. Instead of watching TV, they began to read. Their reason was that TV seemed so out of place in this home, to them, it was almost a sacrilege to watch it.

The front door to the house seemed to resemble what one would imagine if one were to visit a sixteenth century merchant's home. The motif inside had nothing to do with my wife or myself. The house came fully decorated and furnished.

The décor was unusual with its exposed high ceilings, exposed beams, massive staircase, and dark paneled walls. Even the most modern place in the house, the kitchen, had an aura of age about it.

The only room in the house where this sense of décor was violated was the master's bedroom, which was located in the second story, at the end of a long hallway. This was a room that was about 12 feet wide and about 24 feet long, about as wide as the house. You can enter the room through a door from the hallway.

The room had a vaulted ceiling with large decorative beams and paneling that made it look like the inside of a Spanish castle. Across from the door, was a large Spanish window which looked out into a lush forest. When you entered and looked to the left, against the wall, was a four-foot counter with a sink and drawers underneath the counter.

The wall above the counter was covered with a counter to ceiling four-foot mirror. On the wall to the left of the counter, was the door to the bathroom. To the right of the counter, was a built-in closet about five feet wide and eight feet long. The door to the closet was set in that wall next to the counter, and the closet wall that was facing into the room rose to intersect with the vaulted paneled ceiling. That wall was covered, floor to ceiling, with decorative mirrors.

When you look to the left you will see the rest of the room. The wall at the other end of the room was wallpapered with a full-wall mural of a forest scene. The wall with the large Spanish window was covered with plaster and painted beige. The other wall was also covered with plaster and painted beige.

The dressers were placed against the plastered wall with the entrance door, and the bed was placed against the plastered wall with the window opposite the dresser. This worked wonders for one lying in bed; as the forest scene, in all its relaxing serenity, could be seen on the one side giving the illusion of the forest beyond the wall and on the other side, as a beautiful though slightly distorted reflection of that forest.

That forest wall looked so real that it seemed as though you could walk from the room right into it. There were even times when the light spilled into the room, through the large Spanish window, it would seem to be spilling into the room from out of the forest mural. All this was accentuated by the grass green carpet that covered the floor.

When one looked at the house from the outside, it had the appearance of a simple unassuming tri-level house containing approximately eighteen hundred square feet. Once inside though, this house seemed to expand as you moved about, and become a mansion. This illusion seemed to give an underlying ring of truth to the new sign at the entrance to the subdivision, written in Old English Script, announcing *"Magic Forest"*.

The children growing up in this *special environment,* were happy and full of awe as they explored, what seemed to their young minds, this ever expanding and changing house.

We, the parents, were amused by what we overheard them describing it. We attributed these stories to overactive imagination brought about by the shunning of the TV and the reading of too many books. What else could it be?

These stories seemed to center around the master's bedroom with its forested and mirrored walls.

First, they claimed to have seen small animals scurrying about in this forest primeval. Next, it was larger animals. And finally, one spring, a flock of birds. Now this attributing of life to that mural was cute for a while, but enough is enough and these children were becoming a little old to keep playing this game.

We held a family meeting to discuss the oddities taking place in this house, Magic Forest Subdivision, and the behavior of some of the members of this family. Naturally, I, the head of the household, at least as far as the Internal Revenue Service recognizes, brought up the subject of all the animals which were reported to have had inhabited my bedroom for the last eight years. I expected that they would laugh and tell me about the big joke that they had been pulling on me. That wasn't the case though.

They then began to explain how I, too, could see these animals if I only *believed*. If only I was patient enough to wait and watch. A long discussion followed with me forbidding anyone to come into my bedroom to watch the animals. This was seconded by my loyal and loving wife who was also sick of the mess the kids left when they *spent time in our forest*, to use her term.

We, my wife and I, got the kids out of the habit of spending time in our room; and we were pleased, but all of a sudden we found our five cats lying around the room looking hungrily at the forest wall. Now, with the kids, I could understand. I mean, at least they could imagine what they saw, but what was up with the cats?

With the cats came this mess, like little bird droppings here and there around the room.

"The kids have gone too far!" I exclaimed to my wife as I crawled around the dark green carpeted floor trying first to find and then remove the *bird crap*. She only looked back at me with that disinterested smile which told me she would endure my meeting with the kids again, but I was on my own.

The meeting came and went. The bird droppings became worse and the cats became more excited and aggressive. Now, I had more bird droppings plus the damage to the furniture, wall hangings, and drapes caused by the cats. Something had to be done. I decided to call another family meeting and this time I would be tough.

The third family meeting came rather suddenly when one of the cats ate what appeared to be a dead songbird and scattered the remains and feathers all over my sleeping pillow on the bed. I really took charge of this meeting. I ranted, I raved, my wife looked pained, but I made some very good points to back up my contention that this was a practical joke, a darn good one mind you, but a practical joke all the same.

The points were:

1) In eight and a half years living in the house, I had never heard an animal or a bird.

2) I sleep there and have never been awakened or disturbed by anything.

3) The kids got home from school before we got home from work and are in the position to perpetrate this elaborate hoax.

The kids had several suggestions to solve the problem, none of which I felt were practical. My wife reasoned with me and finally persuaded me to follow one suggestion just to show my good faith and open mindedness.

Me, the U.S. Federal Government recognized as head of the household, having to do this stupid thing the kids thought up. Well, anything to keep peace in the family. So here I sat, in a corner made by my dresser and the wall, by the door of the room at 3:30 p.m. wearing my son's sweated-up jogging suit, his deodorant, and his cologne waiting to see what would happen. One by one, as if called to dinner, the five cats entered the room and took up positions on the furniture.

Soon the wall came to life. Birds began to fly from the forest on the wall to the forest reflected in the mirror. It all looked and seemed so real. The cats were going wild jumping and pouncing trying to catch a morsel of food.

I decided that if the movement of the cats didn't scare the birds, I might be able to move to where I could catch a bird, a trophy to show my good and patient wife and the kids. I planned, made my move, and jumped for a bird. I almost had it, but I tripped across the bed and fell so hard into the forest wall; my shoulder broke through the plaster causing the rip in the face of the wall covering. After that episode, the forest settled down and the cats lost interest. I guess I fixed the problem.

That is the story behind that hole in the wall you mentioned. I have had several contractors out to see if they can repair that hole, but none have ever come back to do the job. And I wonder why.

Prescience

Dear Pastor Bob,

During our discussion last evening concerning the strange ways people act, you brought up an interesting question. Would I make the same decision or pursue an alternate course of action if I knew what the outcome would be? We were interrupted before I could answer to that point. Although the story I am going to relate to you will not prove one way or another, it will illustrate to some extent that acting on foreknowledge may or may not always be the answer.

During the time when I was an older student returning to college for my second degree, I was married and lived a considerable distance from the campus. As I lived *off campus* and drove in every day, I was designated as a *commuter student* and assigned to a dorm room which was home to several of my classmates who lived on campus. I became close to one of these fellows and it is his experience with dreams I am about to relate.

It is a scientific fact that everyone must have dreams every night. Experiments have been done where the subjects have been deprived of dream sleep and have behaved in ways different from their normal patterns; therefore, this study concluded that dreams are something we all need to experience.

Some of us remember our dreams when we awake and some of us never remember them at all. Personally, I probably remember 80% of my dreams, and when I recount what happened in them, I can usually question the sanity of the one self that lives its life in the dream state.

My friend also remembered most of his dreams when he awoke in the morning. His major had required him to take a psychology course. He had completed this requirement the previous semester. One of the assignments for this course was that he keeps a detailed dream log. That meant that every morning he should write down the details he could remember from that night's dream or dreams if there were more than one.

Occasionally, when we would all be sitting around kibitzing after class, he would share this log with his roommates and his *commuter roommate*. The most common dream recorded ended something like this, *"and just as I was about to make love to her, the alarm went off."*

He and I had many marketing classes together and we would usually study to prepare for these classes. For one of those classes, our class was divided into groups of two. He and I were one of these groups. Each of these groups were designated as a manufacturing company and our challenge was to market our product in a computer marketing game. He and I had done very well in the market and were leading all the other manufacturers in the game.

Early in the morning of the days the class was in session, we had to enter the results of our days marketing decisions at the computer center at the other end of the campus. It was more convenient for me to drive past the computer center on my morning commute to the dorm than for my roommate to get up early and walk it there. So, I would take the decision home with me each night and drop it off early in the morning the day of the next class.

On this particular Friday morning, after having dropped the decision off at the computer center, I was greeted outside the dorm room by my classmate who was in a most agitated state.

"Thank God, you are alright!" he exclaimed.

"I've never felt better," I answered.

"Is your car alright?" he questioned.

"I don't know, it wasn't talking sense to me this morning, something about a brown Jaguar in a dream last night," I jokingly answered.

"Cut the clowning! I'm serious!" he responded.

"You're always serious about something," I answered.

He more or less ignored my last statement and began again.

"I had a dream...," he was trying to talk.

"You always have dreams! What happened, did you finally catch her?" I cut in.

"No! No! Listen you, clown! This was about an auto wreck, a bad one!" he finally stammered.

Well, knowing the type of dream he usually had from his dream log entries, this sounded quite unusual to me.

"Well...?" I answered.

"And that's not all! Because of that accident, we missed getting our decision to the computer on time and we lost the game!" he emphatically stated as he interrupted me.

I saw how upset he was, and we went into the dorm room to talk. I sat at a desk and he sat at the edge of one of the beds. I had never seen him so upset. We talked some more and it became obvious that we weren't going to make it to our first class, so I remained with him to try to reason with him and to calm him down.

In a nutshell, his dream was vivid. There was an accident. He didn't see the cars, he just knew. The accident was bad enough that there was death and the decision didn't get to the computer center and it cost us.

I first asked him why he was so upset over this dream. Generally, he wrote his dreams down and we laughed at them. Why this dream? His answer made no sense at all, but he was so sincere with his answer that I accepted it at face value. He said that he felt all shook up inside and he just had to share it with me.

We began to analyze his dream.

1. He didn't have a car; therefore, he couldn't have an accident which would delay the decision delivery to the computer center.
2. I had a car and drove every day.
3. I took the decision 35 miles home with me every night and I brought it back 35 miles each morning.
4. If he doesn't have a car and I do, then it must be my car which is about to become a candidate for some junkyard.
5. It appears that on Monday we may lose our lead in the marketing game.

I wasn't happy with this analysis, but at the time, who was I to refute it?

During a free period, we searched out his Psychology Professor from his last semester class and explained to him the problem. He was the perfect example of that old adage: *"those who can't succeed in their fields teach"*. I don't know what it was he couldn't do in life that forced him into teaching, but he couldn't articulate a straight sentence or a straight answer.

"It could mean this........., or it could mean that .... In your state of agitation......," he stuttered.

We finally left the Professor. After our marketing class, we talked it over and decided I would drive carefully, and he would keep the decision over the weekend in our room and walk it over to the computer center Monday morning. We would meet at the usual time in our dorm room and all would be well.

Monday morning, I arrived at the dorm room a little early having encountered no unusual traffic incidents on the way. When I got there, the dorm room was empty. I thought for a minute and concluded that my classmate was late walking back from the computer center. I waited for him as long as I could and then left for my first class. He didn't show up for any of our classes that morning.

At noon, I rushed back to the dorm room to find one of our other roommates. I arrived there just as one was leaving for his next class. He told me he had just received a phone call from our roommate. Our roommate was okay, but he was in a hospital in a neighboring state and being released later that day. He expected to be back in school the next day.

When everything settled down, and we had a chance to talk, I found out that my roommate had a friend from his hometown who was also attending our school. On Saturday morning, this friend contacted him with the news that my roommate's ex girlfriend would be getting married that evening and if they hurried, they could attend the wedding and still be back on campus Sunday night.

This person had a new fast Corvette and there was no question that they would easily make the trip. My roommate grabbed some clothes and his briefcase, so he could study on the way and they were off.

Sunday evening, they got a late start coming back. And at 2:00 a.m. on Monday morning they hit a deer demolishing that pretty, *plastic* car. They were both taken to the local hospital for observation.

Can you believe it? The dream was fulfilled. The deer died and the decision was not delivered on Monday morning. The facts of the story are the easy part. The hard part is to question what really took place and how the various parts of the dream were related. For the sake of discussion, I will pose these questions,

1. What was the purpose of the dream? Was it a warning of the accident? Or of the decision being late?
2. Was it that the decision would be late? And this would be caused by an accident?
3. Was this pre-ordained and the decision would have been late no matter what happened?

If we consider situation number 1, then we must assume that my roommate was warned that he was going to have an accident which would result in the decision being late. Had we left well enough alone, and not meddled in what was pre-ordained, I would have brought in the decision and he would have had his accident.

If we consider situation number 2, then we must assume that my roommate was warned that the decision would be late and by trying to meddle in this pre-ordained situation we changed the accident from happening to my car to happening to his friend's car.

If we consider situation number 3, we must question whether missing the deadline on the decision was pre-ordained and no matter what we would have done, would have had no effect on which accident actually occurred.

Maybe this was all just a coincidence that this dream came true. No matter how we look at this, we will never know it. Even if one knows the outcome of a situation ahead of time, or if one changes the conditions, or the players, will the outcome be changed or will it always end up the same? Even with that story, the question is still unanswered.

The Coffin Trip

Dear Pastor Bob,

Over the years, I have appreciated the way we have been able to share our faith experiences and learn from them. We have talked many times about how The Lord uses circumstances to prepare us for those times when we need to be helpful to another person. This Holiday Season, another one of those situations arose.

The week before Christmas was a short work week. I felt satisfied that I had ended my travels for the year on a high note. Then in the middle of the week, I received a phone message from my distributor in Roanoke, Virginia. I returned the call to the manager to find out what he needed. His request was that I hold a two-day product sales training meeting during the week between Christmas and New Years.

This was really good news. I had been trying to arrange this meeting to go over new products for some months, with no success. This was because his outside salesmen needed to attend, but there wasn't a time when all of them could be called out of the field at the same time. Now, during the Holidays, they would all be available.

I jumped at the chance and immediately made the necessary plane, rental car, and motel reservations. I would be traveling mid-week between Christmas Day and New Year's Eve. This should really put a cap on my good year.

As trips go, this one seemed pretty much cut and dried, a simple two-day sales meeting. I went to bed happy, but alas when I awakened the next morning, I had an uneasy feeling about this flight. This was a feeling of foreboding bordering, maybe even a feeling of outright fear. I didn't know what it was, but whatever it was it weighed me down. As the week progressed, the weight of this concern became heavier and began to focus.

The best way I can describe this was, it focused my mind on death and I began to fear making that plane flight into the Roanoke airport. Each day, the feelings became more intense, and yet my sense of reason was telling me that this was foolishness. Flying was safe and I couldn't cancel the trip for a sales meeting I had been trying to get for months just because of an irrational fear; I just couldn't give in to my fears.

I prayed about the trip. I asked guidance for the trip. I was looking for an answer, and my way seemed clear. I must go, but my fear would not subside. I talked to my wife. I didn't give her all the details of my fear, just a little, enough for her to give me insight into her feelings. Again, I got no direction, the trip was still on.

By this time, this *thing* had become so large in my mind that even Christmas Eve and Sunday services couldn't overshadow my feelings. My feelings had become a foreboding of death. I pondered deeply on the question of just why I was doing this. I had no answer, except that it was my job, and I enjoyed the travel and it was how I feed my family.

My flight was Tuesday at noon. I vowed to spend as much time as I could with my family and we had a good Christmas Eve. My wife was even impressed with the gift I gave her. I prayed a lot in church on Sunday. And Sunday afternoon with the kids was wonderful and Monday evening was very good also.

My trip to the airport and my checking in for the flight took placed without incident. I went to the kiosk and took out extra insurance for the flight to Roanoke. This was unusual as I never did that. It is strange what one does when his future seems threatened. And yet, I was so calm about the whole thing. If I were going to meet The Lord, I was ready. And I guess, for whom I was about to meet, I was also thoroughly prepared.

I boarded the plane without incident. I wasn't happy with my seat assignment, but it was too late to change it. So, there I was in row 16, seat C waiting to fly. I placed my carry-on bag in the overhead bin, my briefcase under my seat and, as I usually did, settled into my seat.

Sitting comfortably in the seat, I bowed my head, said a prayer, and felt really foolish about my fears of the last few days. I looked up and turned my head to look out the window. When I board the plane early, I sometimes have the opportunity to watch the baggage handlers abuse my luggage as they load it into the belly of the plane. This time, a large box or container caught my attention as it was carefully being loaded into the belly of the plane. I had seen this take place before and recognized the box as a coffin. I wondered about where it was being shipped to. I turned my head and looked up the aisle. Coming down the aisle were two young ladies.

The one leading the way was dressed in a conservative dark suit with a white blouse. Her hair was a dark color, medium length, and permed in a style reminiscent of the early 1960s. She wore very little makeup, but what she wore was smeared as though she had been crying. Her eyes appeared bloodshot.

The woman following her wore a dark dress either dark blue or black. She carried a tan overcoat. Her blond hair was long and stringy. Her face was as white as death. Her eyes were dark and sunken as though she had also been crying.

Somehow when I looked up, I ended up looking directly into the eyes of the first young lady. There was something about the way she looked at me that held my gaze. I couldn't look away. She continued to hold my gaze as she came down the aisle towards my seat.

"Excuse me please!" she said, "I am in seat 16D."

"Just a moment." I answered, as I unbuckled my seatbelt and got up out of my seat and stood in the aisle to let her pass.

"You go first." she said to the lady behind her, and the lady who looked like death took the seat by the window. The first lady then claimed the seat next to mine. I sat back down and refastened my seatbelt.

Stories Told by Traveling Salesmen

I have always enjoyed talking with lovely ladies when I sit next to them in an airplane, and I usually have ways of beginning a conversation with them. This, however, was the exception. The lady seated next to the window was totally absorbed in her own thoughts, staring into and through the seatback in front of her. The lady beside me was looking intently into her lap where she was continually and nervously twisting her folded hands.

I looked over at the two silent ladies and concluded this looked as though it would be a quiet trip, as I probably wouldn't be able to strike up a conversation with them. I figured I would settle down in the seat and catch a nap. This plan was interrupted when the airline captain announced, over the speaker system, that the flight would be delayed.

Out of the corner of my eye, I noticed that the lady seated next to me had stopped wringing her hands. She was now nervously moving wedding rings back and forth on the ring finger of her left hand. She appeared very nervous.

"Do you fly often?" I asked, thinking that I might be able to lessen her anxiety.

"No," she stiffly replied.

"These people run a pretty safe airline," I volunteered, thinking that by that statement I might lessen her fears, because with the way they acted, she and her friend must be panic-stricken about flying. I thought that if I could get them talking maybe they would relax a little.

"How far are you going?" I questioned.

The plane made one more stop after Roanoke and I thought this question might break the ice.

"Just to Roanoke," she replied, her answer coming from a place as cold and hard as I had ever experienced. She continued to sit there playing with the wedding rings on her ring finger.

I pulled my briefcase out from under my seat, opened it, and got something to work on, closed it, and pushed it back where it had come from. I positioned my tray table, so I could write and began to read what I was working on. After all, who knew how long we would sit here at the gate. Once the plane was airborne, I could then take a little nap.

"Are you on business?" the lady beside me asked in a very cold and accusative way.

"Yeah," I replied more or less in an *I-don't-want-to-be-bothered-now* type of voice. With her attitude problems I began to think talking to her was not in my best interest.

"What do you do?" was her next question.

"I sell," I answered.

That answer brought a long pause in our conversation.

I began writing some memo or something for work. I noticed she was still playing with her wedding ring set.

"Do you have a family?" she sharply asked, breaking my concentration.

"Yeah," I answered, "a wife and four kids."

"Are you on your way home for New Year's?" she asked in an even more accusing tone of voice.

"No, I am on my way to Roanoke to hold a two-day sales training session beginning tomorrow," I replied.

Her next question was very hard for her to ask and she kind of sobbed as she asked it. "Why aren't you home with your wife and family during this Holiday Season?"

"Because my distributor needs me now," I replied as I turned to face her.

She looked at me and I saw tears welling up in her eyes. She was giving me a hard glaring look of deep disapproval.

The stewardess came by to check on our seatbelts and to remind me to raise and lock my tray table. The plane came to life and soon we were air born. I lowered my tray table and returned to the work before me. It took enough time for me to regain my train of thoughts about what I was working on before she addressed me again.

"Why do you do it?" she asked in a demanding voice.

"Do what?" I asked.

"Leave your wife and travel," she coldly replied.

"It's what I do," I answered.

With this answer from me, she was quiet for a while. She began sobbing and the hardness seemed to begin to break away. Then she spoke as if asking me, but not really, "Why did he have to go, why, why, why?" she questioned as if speaking to no one.

Then she turned to face me.

I really didn't know how to respond, so I asked,

"Were you speaking to me?"

If I continued writing this as it was spoken, it would take several tablets of paper and would be long and boring to read. As her story unfolded, I realized that the worry and agony I experienced during the last week had prepared me to talk with her on this trip.

But this is getting ahead of the story, you see, her trip was one of deep sorrow. It happened this way.

Some years ago, she had met this man down in Houston, Texas. He was from Salem, Virginia, and she was from a little town in that part of Missouri that juts down into Arkansas. They dated, fell in love, and eventually were married. They made their home in one of the Houston suburbs. They had put off having a family until her paycheck wouldn't be needed anymore. He traveled mostly in Texas close to the Houston area, so he didn't have to spend many nights a month out on the road.

Living in Houston, so far from her folks and his, they hadn't visited either set of relatives very often. They had met each other's parents for the first time at the wedding and over the past few years had only visited each of the families a couple of times. That is why this Christmas was going to be so special. He never had a lot of business to take care of over the Holidays, so they had arranged to have three weeks off from work this year.

This meant that there would be time enough to visit her folks for Christmas and his folks for New Year's. For once, they would have real family celebrations for the Holidays. His unmarried sister, who lived in Kansas City, Missouri, had joined her in Houston and would drive with them for the whole trip.

"Oh, it was going to be so wonderful!"

Everything went according to plan. The weekend before Christmas they left Houston for the nice leisurely two-day drive to Missouri. And they arrived Sunday afternoon. Sunday night couldn't have been better. Then on Monday afternoon, his factory called. There were problems at a customer's plant with one of the products he sold, and it couldn't wait. How fast could he get there? Well, the plant was near Dallas, and was about a good day's drive if he went through Little Rock. And if he started tonight, he might be there Tuesday noon.

He made the drive. He called her every night. He missed her very much, but it was taking longer than anticipated. It should be done, so he should be able to drive back Christmas Eve Day. He had called her at 4:00 p.m. Christmas Eve's day to tell her he was done with the job and on the road. He told her that if he took some back roads through Arkansas, he could save some miles and he should be home to her by midnight.

At 8:30 p.m. he had called again. He was behind schedule and was still somewhere in Arkansas, but he was making up time. He thought 3:00 a.m. would be a good arrival time and she should not worry.

At 9:30 p.m. on Christmas eve, the Arkansas Highway Patrol Officer phoned her to tell her that her husband had been in an automobile accident and had given them her number before he died.

She and his sister, who was sitting beside her, were accompanying the body home to Salem for burial in the family plot. Her question to me was very pointed and she kept asking it,

"Why did he have to go? Why did he have to travel?"

Now, who is better prepared than a traveling salesman, could explain something this complicated to anybody.

When she had taken a moment to regain her composure, she repeated her question again,

"Why did he have to travel?" And then she looked me square in the eyes and demanded, "Why do you travel?"

It was strange, but that was one of the very questions I had asked myself last week. After much self-searching and reflection, I had come up with an answer which satisfied me. I now began to share this answer with her.

"Some people are born satisfied and live their whole life never venturing too far from the known, the comfortable, or the mundane. Some are born curious and although they question and explore, they never break the bonds that keep them shackled to their ordered and structured life. Then there are those born restless. Those rare individuals who society, try as it might, never can be made to conform exactly to the norm."

"These are the people who go over the next hill for no other reason than to see what is on the other side. These are the ones with the '*itchy feet*'. The only time the feet don't itch is when they are moving."

"It is sometimes thought, among the mundane thinkers in society, that with the proper incentive, these people can someday be made to conform. Many have lived dreary existences placed in confinement by these incentives, always wishing, always dreaming, but never able to fulfill their restless urges."

"Some of these become wanders, bums if you like, hippies or artists. Some of these beings are born with a special talent. These become '*Traveling Salesmen*' and are actually paid to roam around and talk to people. These are the ones who derive great pleasure from going where the action is, from being in the middle of the solution of a problem, and from driving from call to call drinking in the beauty of the day while doing that."

As we talked, she began to see, in this description, the very things within him which had made him so special to her. The very things that made him the one she loved.

We talked about duty. What it is within a man that would force him to take time away from his family, to breakup his vacation, to leave her, and go to work on a job.

Was it the restless part of him getting out? Was it the part of him trying to conform to the norms of society? Or was it his commitment to his product and his customers? Through all the discussion we had, we really never answered this.

The question; for her *"why he had to travel"* was really another underlying question in disguise. The real question nagging her mind was, *"Did he travel because he really didn't love me"*. By the way she phrased some of her questions about my relationship with my wife, I think she wanted to make sure that I was not traveling to get away from my wife.

That my wife was not the reason I traveled. I explained that my dedication to my traveling was also for the benefit of my wife and family. That the money I earned was necessary to keep the roof over our heads and that there were times I really would have liked to remain home, but for my sense of duty I made the trip. And that at times it was a sacrifice for the family.

By the time the plane landed in Roanoke, I had spent nearly two hours with her addressing questions to me, questions that she had never addressed to her husband. Here, I was answering them for her as one who did what her husband had done.

During the whole trip, we never had the opportunity to discuss his outlook on life or if he had a Christian faith. I guess that was to be left up to those on the ground waiting for the plane. Yet, before we parted, I gave her some words of consolation and said a short prayer. I deplaned, took my carry-on to the rental desk, and left the airport. I never saw the two ladies again.

My fear and foreboding had evaporated as though a weight had been lifted from my shoulders. Deep down I knew that last week's wondering and all I had gone through had been training and preparing me for this ride. My job on Tuesday had been to share some of my deepest feelings with a stranger, so she could settle in her own mind why her man traveled and did what he did.

The rest of the trip went without incident and as you guessed, I am writing this from my desk at home.

Requiem

Art Kaufman picked up the rental car at the airport in the small southern coastal city. He had made the usual reservation through ABC Rentals for a sub-compact car. His plan was to drop it three days later at the airport in the big city. Naturally, he was to be charged the usual $45.00 drop-off charge for the privilege. The traveling man rarely wins in this rental game. Sure, he got the big Lincoln for the price of the sub-compact, but at what cost?

This car is going home to its base and Art is paying $45.00 for the privilege of returning it there. Of course, there is also the extra cost of the gas it will burn. The extra cost hurts, but one could get over that, it was the smell in this car that wouldn't go away. Some hick must have driven this car with manure on his shoes.

Sure, Art complained and tried to get another car from ABC Rental, but to no avail. Yes, they would give him another car, but he would have to wait until one came in and none were scheduled until evening. By this time, Art was already going to be late for his first call due to this rental car problem, and he wouldn't be passing this way again for some time in the normal course of his route. He just would have to put up with this *shit*.

The sun was beginning to set, and Art was still on the road to the next major city where his guaranteed late arrival at the motel awaited him. He hadn't been gone from home for 12 hours yet, but home was 705 miles away by his calculations. By now, Patience, his wife, would have coaxed the little ones into bed and would be helping the older one with homework, or maybe they would be playing a game. Art had to fight it. It was too early in the week to be missing Patience and the kids already.

His mind wandered to the four calls he had made that day. Three were good calls and he had at least obtained engineering commitments for his products from them. One of the good calls was okay, but the person he needed to see had broken the appointment. Although he had talked with the man's personal secretary, he felt he had not achieved the best result. He would have to come back to close the deal. The last call was the loser, and he had spent the most time with this account.

He knew he was right and that his Engineering Data was without flaw, but this older engineer had always done things another way and a competitor had gotten to him and reinforced the old way first. Now Art was, so to speak, sucking hind tit.

The darker it got, the slower this road seemed to be passing under the car. Art had set the speed control and was trying to carefully watch the road. Some large ship must have docked at the southern port because the trucks hauling containers seemed to be dominating this northbound stretch of interstate.

Art played with the radio. The AM band had nothing but down-home country music. Art tried the FM band, nothing there but a little Jazz and more Country Western. He tried the FM Dial from 89.0 to 90.9 where National Public Radio stations usually were located to try for classical music, but he was still out of range from them. The trucks around him had become thicker.

The radio went off with the click of a switch. If only that sweet young lady with those two little children had not been on the plane. Seeing a family like that always accelerated the lonely feelings that Art got when he traveled.

"*How do you get those thoughts out of your mind? You don't!*" he thought.They will always be a part of you, and you will always miss them. It just didn't have to start so soon in the trip. Oh, the sweet sensuous kiss Art remembered from his sendoff at 5:00 a.m. that morning.

Art would like to take Patience on the road once in a while, but with the little kids at home, it was impossible. They would have to get a babysitter which would cost a fortune, then would have to come up with the extra plane fare the company wouldn't cover and the other expenses.

Art's dream was broken. There was a container truck in front of the Lincoln, one at the back, and the one beside him was moving into his lane. He pressed the brakes softly, but the container truck at the back gave no inch.

"Oh shit!" exclaimed Art as he pulled onto the shoulder off the road and swerved into the ditch out of the way. "What the devil did I do to piss them off?" he asked himself.

He was driving with his speed control set at 57 miles per hour. If only he had a CB radio, he could find out what he had done to offend the three drivers he had just encountered.

Getting back on the road and up to speed was no problem for the Lincoln. He did notice, however, that he was gaining on those three eighteen-wheelers. He also noticed that he seemed to be the only four-wheeler he could see anywhere on his side of the interstate in either direction. He had to be careful though as he was still gaining on those three eighteen-wheelers.

Later, it seemed as though they were pacing him because they were still in a configuration that would not allow him to pass and yet as they approached each of the hills they were slowing. If he continued at this pace, he was going to have a hard time avoiding them. The next road sign announced exit 36 one mile. Art pulled off at that exit and felt less intimidated and a whole lot safer.

The Quick Stop had coffee and a stale sweet roll, probably left over from the morning, yet it hit the spot. If only country music wasn't playing in the background.

The Lincoln accelerated up the entrance ramp onto the expressway, *still at least an hour to go.* The Country music playing in the background at the Quick Stop had brought back the loneliness that the adrenaline stimulated by the truck drivers had masked. If there was ever some type of music that made Art lonely, it was that darn Country and Western. It spoke to him of loneliness, unfaithful love, heartbreak, and death.

None of those feelings uplifted him; they only made him feel worse. He checked the radio again for the National Public Radio station and through the static he found it. The Minneapolis Philharmonic was playing something. Whatever it was, it soothed him, and he drove awake and alert the rest of the way to his motel.

It was 9:45 when he reached his motel. The odor still hadn't left the rental car, but apparently it hadn't accumulated on his clothes and shoes as no one in the lobby seemed to notice the smell. There was no problem at check in. The proper form was signed; the American Express Card was passed back and forth, and the room number was assigned.

Art was meticulous about always requesting, in his reservation, that his room be *down and out* on the first floor with parking in front. He did this because of the luggage and sample cases he carried. Usually, if he got to the motel early enough, he had a good chance of getting the room he requested. It was already 9:45 and the desk clerk had obviously given all the *"down and outs"* to the early arrivals.

He knew from experience that to argue was in vain, but he couldn't help stopping to point out that he made his reservation two weeks before and he felt that he deserved consideration for the room he had requested. Of course, the desk clerk was quick to point out that all the first floor rooms were holdovers and there was no way he could have gotten his request fulfilled that night anyway. As he left, Art was overheard muttering something about stories and lying, but that was only to let off steam.

The room was typical. It had two beds against one wall with a common nightstand furniture piece hanging on the wall between them. Above the nightstand, on either side, were reading lights attached to the wall so that they could be used while lying in bed. The nondescript headboards were accented by the cheap, mass-produced, modernistic pictures which were centered above each headboard and fastened to the wall with screws through the picture frame.

The air conditioner or heater was under the drapery covered window at the door end of the room. Between it and a bed, was a round table surrounded by three chairs. Above the table hang, what has in better times, been called a hanging lamp but has lately been referred to as a swag or chain lamp. Along the wall were the low dressers on which the sat TV. Art used one of these as a place to open and unpack his suitcase. Past the bed on this side of the room was an opening to the bathroom area.

Art carried the first load up the staircase to his room and opened the door. The suitcase went on one of the dressers and the briefcase went on the round table. With his second load, the sample cases arrived and were placed in a corner out of his way. Now, he followed his routine, locked and chained the motel door from the inside.

It was 10:15 by the time he had himself settled in the room, and he finally got to the outside telephone line to call Patience. His call was an hour and a quarter late. She would have worried a little, but she as always, sounded happy to hear his voice. They exchanged news and after each told the other how much they were missed, he hung up.

He was hungry and considered going out to find something to eat. He gave that up as the only places where he would be able to find hot food would be small, greasy, spoon-type joints; and although the food might sooth the stomach now, it would cause heartburn which would not be worth it later. It might have kept him up all night. Art turned on the TV for company, catching the end of Cagney and Lacy, and opened his briefcase on the table to check some things for tomorrow's calls.

The news was over, his teeth were brushed, and he had silenced the TV. He reached up and turned out the light at the head of the bed. And as he lay there in the dark, he counted the ticking of his alarm clock on the nightstand. He told himself he must sleep, but Patience and the kids kept coming up in his mind. It was for times like these he kept the family picture in his wallet. He turned on the light and he studied the pictures for a short time.

Art was not much of a religious man, but he did know what a Bible was and this night, after saying a little prayer, he read himself to sleep. A while later, he awakened enough to see the Bible had slipped from his hand and fallen to the floor. He was too tired to even move it. He reached up and turned out the light.

The alarm went off right in the middle of the dream, it had an unidentified woman in it, and she was seducing him. He had many mornings when his libido would be building to a peak right at the time the alarm would sound. If he were at home, Patience would be there beside him. He would place his arm over her soft sleeping body and kind of hug her awake. The warm morning embrace which would follow would remain with him for the rest of the day.

The cold reality was that he was not at home, but in a cold motel room and he probably better take a cold shower. For some salesmen, the next night would be a night of sexual adventure in some bar or Western Music dance hall. For Art, it would be lonely, filled with paperwork. He used the time away from home to do things that would free up his weekend. As he did this, he would dream of the time during the weekend when he felt free to *do something with the family.*

Art stepped out of the shower and dried himself with one of the towels from the rack on the wall. He looked at his watch, deciding that at 7:00 a.m., the Today Show should be on the tube and proceeded to tune it in. The news was on while he pulled on his underwear. He went to the suitcase and chose a beige pair of trousers and a navy-blue blazer to wear along with the pinstriped shirt. He reached into a pocket of the suitcase and pulled out a pair of black socks. He pulled on his trousers, sat on the edge of the bed to pull on his socks and reached for his shirt.

Art was meticulous and it was at this time he remembered he had missed brushing his teeth and shaving. Back to the bathroom he went, got his shaver ready and began top run water. A blade always works best with the hottest possible water. While he was running water, he placed toothpaste on the bristles of the toothbrush. He was probably distracted concentrating on something about the weather on the tube.

If he even heard the key in the lock of his motel room, it is uncertain. Art probably heard the safety chain being ripped from the door frame causing shattering of the wood into which it was fastened. He didn't have time to shave or brush his teeth.

It was 9:00 a.m. when the maid tried the door to the room, found it unlocked and the room in disorder. By 9:30 the police had determined that his ABC Rental car was missing, as was his wallet and a few things from his sample case.

It was 5:30 p.m. when a fisherman on his way down a dirt road to a private lake in a neighboring state found the remains. From the investigator's report, it was determined that he had been found hands tied behind his back, dressed in underwear, beige trousers with no belt, and black socks. There was no identification on the body, but something found in a pocket traced to his motel. From the stains on the knees of his trousers, it appeared he had been kneeling when he was shot, at the base of the skull from behind, execution style. The rental car was not found at the scene.

It was about 9:00 p.m. when Patience heard the phone ring.

"Well, at least tonight he will tell me had a good day, she said excitedly to herself. He is calling on time." And she had so much to tell him.

The voice on the phone was strange. The questions were unusual."Yes, this is the residence of Art Kaufman. No, he isn't home. He is away on a sales trip. The Police? You say he has been found?"

The crime made the next day's paper, but it had no warning to any other traveling man, although this had happened to several of late. It appeared on a middle page in a three column, five-inch story with a headline, "*Salesman from Out of Town Murdered Yesterday.*" The article was vague, giving no details. The city was used to this kind of news.

And a week later, the city forgot.

Author notes: This story is in memory of a close associate who met an untimely death while traveling on the road.

Witch Hazel's Broom

You have questioned me tonight as to why we are driving the rental car from Fort Lauderdale to Jacksonville, FL, a six-hour drive up I-95, when we could have so easily just gotten a ride on one of those little commuter airplanes. I refer to those little commuter airplanes as Witch Hazel's Broom so you will know what I mean if later I mention that phrase.

We could very well have flown, but the cost would have been greater than the mileage charge for this rental car. I could have further justified this trip for you by saying the drive to the airport from where our last call was would have taken at least an hour. The rental car return would have taken at least 30 minutes. We would have had to be there an hour early to buy our tickets and take care of our luggage.

The plane being smaller would have taken at least two and a half hours to make the flight. Claiming our luggage and getting the rental car would have taken at least an hour. The bottom line is that we would have spent a lot more money just to save one hour of non-working travel time. The justification I could make would be that, this drive is more economical.

The real reason I have chosen to drive goes back many years. We have enough driving time, so I will use a little of it to tell you that story.

When I was younger and more energetic than I am now, when the company had the need, I was more than happy to spread myself thin and manage a double territory. I usually did this until someone could be hired and allow me to concentrate solely on my own territory again. In those days, a good new challenge was almost as good as getting a raise.

Then, as is now, part of my territorial responsibility was to work with the established distribution network and the other part was to find and work with Original Equipment Manufacturers. The goal was to enhance the quality of their product by using, within their product, the component part we could provide. The search for these small manufacturers brought me into many out-of-the-way little towns.

I had driven my rental car to Monroe, Louisiana from a sales meeting with my distributor in Shreveport to visit a small manufacturing company the next morning. This company was making small air compressors. I had been negotiating with them to complete an OEM (*Original Equipment Manufacturer*) agreement. I had been working on this with them for many months. My original intent was to finish my meetings that morning, drive back to Shreveport to turn in the rental car, and fly home to Atlanta. This was my last trip before the Christmas Holidays, and I needed the time to prepare for them.

When you travel and spend three to four nights per week away from home, the pressure becomes greater to be home with the wife to help with the kids, especially during the Holidays. This trip, which came up suddenly, was only agreed to by the better half on the promise that *nothing* would keep me from returning home on a prescribed day. I remember that conservation as if it were yesterday.

"If you are not home by Wednesday evening, you won't find me and the kids here when you do get here!"

I had it all planned down to the last 5 minutes and the Braniff Flight Schedule.

Monday – Atlanta – Shreveport, Rental car at airport.
    Meeting with distributor 11:00 to 3:00 p.m.
    Drive to Monroe – Spend the night.

Tuesday – Meeting at 9:00 a.m. until 2:00 p.m.
  Drive back to Shreveport
  Catch plane if early enough, spend night if not.
Wednesday – If not at home catch plane to Atlanta in the morning
  Arrive home in time to make wife happy.

That was the plan.

You don't travel the south, so you ask why drive to Monroe when you could have just as well flown. I have two answers for that question. First, to fly from Shreveport to Monroe roundtrip you had to use commuter airlines, and they used what were known then as light twin aircraft. Secondly, the rainy, stormy weather in Louisiana in December made riding in a 727 seem risky at best and even in my younger days, I only rode commuter airlines in good weather.

My plan was working well. I arrived at the Monroe Factory fifteen minutes early. I checked in with the receptionist. She told me the man I was to meet was attending a certain Christmas Function with his children at a certain Parochial school and had postponed our meeting. The one I had fought with my wife over. He wouldn't be able to see me until 3:00 p.m. that day.

She added, "He hopes you understand, it being family and all."

I graciously told the receptionist that I would return at 3:00 p.m. for our meeting. I left to find a phone to do a little business in the meantime.

I phoned some accounts to follow up on quotes and checked in with the factory. My boss, the V.P. of Sales and Marketing, impressed upon me how important this account could be and how he knew my dedication was such that I would see this meeting brought the desired commitment, etc. I phoned Delta Air Lines and changed my Braniff flight to a Delta morning one the next day and was all set.

At 2:45 I arrived in the reception area and claimed a chair. I found a stack of Compressed Air Magazines on the coffee table in front of me. I began to look at articles concerning various new uses for compressed air. It was probably 3:15 when I asked the receptionist if my contact was ready to see me yet. She said she would check. Nothing happened until about 4:45 when I overheard a conversation.

The receptionist was speaking on the phone in hushed tones. Now, I don't know about you, but when I am sitting in a reception area and the receptionist or switchboard operator talks loudly the whole time I am there, I tune her out. Now, if I am the only one in the reception area and all of a sudden the receptionist begins to talk very softly, I perk up my ears and listen intently because nine times out of ten the conversation concerns something I am not supposed to overhear.

"He's been here since 3:00 at least ....no I didn't ...... yes sir, I'll tell him."

Now I looked at my watch and guessed what I was about to hear,

"That was Mr. ------. He told me to tell you he was sorry he couldn't make it this afternoon, because his wife insisted that he stay for the social and all. He hopes you'll understand! He promised he will be back to see you at 10:30 tomorrow morning."

Well I understood all right. He could have his family and do his special things with them while I had to jump at his request and incur the wrath of mine.

"I'll be back at 10:00," I told her and left.

Back to the motel, check back in. It was the Christmas Holidays – sure they had a lot of room. I kill another night in a motel and miss just a little bit more of the Christmas Spirit. I phoned Delta to change my reservations again and see what the agent on the phone could think of to help.

"Why yes, we can connect you out of Monroe through New Orleans. I can book you on a flight on this little feeder airline, it's called ******** at 1:30 p.m. to arrive New Orleans at 3:00, you pick up Delta at 3:55 and arrive Atlanta at 7:30 p.m. No problem," and she booked the flight.

Fortunately, the costs for all this would be picked up by the company, but my boss wouldn't be happy.

The Hertz rental agent was gracious and told me what the drop-off charges would be, but it all got arranged.

I phoned my wife, who hadn't lost any of her insistence as to where I was to be Wednesday night. I didn't even tell her how the day had gone or ask for more time. In the mood she was in, she just might have packed the kids and left early.

Now the plans were made, the pressure was off. It had fallen into place and I would make it home. Good sign I thought as I relaxed in the motel room after dinner. Tomorrow should go well, I will get the agreement signed and my boss will be happy.

10:00 a.m. found me cooling my heels in the reception area I had come to know so well the day before. Earlier, I had spoken with my boss on the phone and filled him in on what had taken place. He sounded very encouraging. I drove to the airport and purchased the necessary tickets.

I looked at the light twin airplane parked at the ramp and really couldn't believe this small airplane was the one. If there hadn't been such pressure to get home, I would never have agreed to do this. In my mind, because of its size, I dubbed it *"Witch Hazel's Broom"*.

Finally, at 11:00, I got my audience with Mr. _____ . *Great*. I picked up my briefcase and was ushered into his office. I opened my briefcase, took out the folder with the agreement in it and prepared to talk business.

The first fifteen minutes was devoted to small talk, well, not exactly, as it took him that long to describe how his brilliant kids had stolen the show at yesterday's pageant.

I opened my folder to discuss the project and the OEM Agreement with him. He suggested we do that on a full stomach and catch an early lunch. As he could not be dissuaded, I went with him.

At the restaurant we *ran into* some of his friends from town and I ended up buying them some Christmas cheer. I bought him Christmas lunch and it was already 1:05 p.m. when we reached his office. I wasn't a dying man, but I began seeing my marriage, my kids, my family, my divorce, and my financial ruin passing before my eyes.

Stories Told by Traveling Salesmen

Back in his office, I opened my briefcase and brought out the agreement for him to sign explaining that I had a 1:30 flight to catch and we had to wrap this up fast.

Finally, he got serious and answered,

"Oh, didn't I tell you, our corporate lawyers in New York feel that your company's product might incur added liability problems if the units were misused. They have forbidden incorporating your product into ours."

I thanked him for the opportunity of taking him to lunch, asked him to put his last statement into writing, shook his hand and left. The time now was 1:20 and I had to get to the airport to ride Witch Hazel's Broom.

It was so close to 1:30 when the rental car got to the airport. I thought I was going to see the plane leave as I pulled up. I parked in front of the airport entrance, grabbed my briefcase, and my suitcase and dashed into the airport up to the ticket counter.

The lady who had sold me the ticket earlier that morning smiled, took my bag and said, "You are our only passenger today, so we waited for you. Didn't want to fly empty, you know."

I wheeled the car into the Hertz Company parking lot, gave the keys to the Hertz attendant and left asking that he mail my copy of the contract.

Witch Hazel's Broom was finally loaded with its one passenger. Ground clearance was given, and I was airborne at approximately 1:37 p.m.

This seemed to be working out quite well. I was going to be home in time and it looked as though this flight might be fun. I normally sit in the back-row seats in the planes I fly. You haven't heard of any airplanes backing into any mountains lately, have you Me, being the only passenger in a light twin, decided to move up and sit directly behind the co-pilot. I have always been fascinated with flying and I usually don't have the opportunity to look through the windshield of any airplane. Unfortunately, there wasn't much to see as the weather

Alan M. Oberdeck

was stormy and we were flying on top of the cloud layer, where the air was smoother.

We were probably 30 miles from New Orleans Airport, and I was listening to the co-pilot speaking into the microphone communicating with someone, probably the airport tower. Mostly, he was looking at the gages in front of him and discussing our position and any surrounding air traffic. As far as I could see, there were no surrounding aircraft. He was adjusting knobs in front of him to give us our bearing.

All of a sudden, out of the blue a blinding flash appeared, and the plane began to shake and vibrate violently. The pilot immediately cut power and some of the violent shaking stopped. Luckily, I was belted in or I could have gotten hurt. The first thing I noticed when things settled down was that the co-pilot was frantically trying to get a response from the aircraft controllers over the radio. Finally, the pilot flipped a switch and the controller's response was heard over the speaker system. That gave me confidence that we at least had communication with the ground.

Being able to hear the conservation allowed me to follow the unfolding of our dilemma. The lightning and the severe turbulence had caused some kind of damage to the plane's electrical system and only one radio worked, no transponder, no VOR, and nothing electrical of that nature worked.

Here, we were between two layers of clouds unable to safely break through them and find the airport. Here, we were caught layers during a storm on the ground just flying squares in the sky trying to burn off fuel. With the transponder and encoding altimeter not working, we could only guess where we were, and the controllers on the ground didn't know for sure either. Lost, between the clouds, Witch Hazel's Broom wasn't doing too well.

While we circled, the pilot tried in vain to find the one fuse or electrical connection which would restore the power we needed. The co-pilot read the compass headings and altitude to the controllers on the ground, and there was still nothing. We were still between the cloud layers holding our own, hoping the pilot could remedy the situation. When the pilot took out a road map and commented to the co-pilot that he had hoped he would never have to use it to find a rice paddy to land in. He began to study that map.

Suddenly, one of the controllers was heard on the radio.

"Inbound Delta flight number 1003 has spotted what he thinks might be your plane. He asks that you make a two-minute turn to see if it is your plane he sees."

The co-pilot immediately acknowledged, and the pilot began our turn. Soon, we caught sight of the large jet in the distance,

"Confirmation on visual of Delta 1003," the co-pilot radioed back.

"Confirmation from Delta on your identification. Please continue to fly as you have, so we can determine your position and place you in a safe spot."

"Roger," the co-pilot replied.

The discussion continued with the controller on the ground and we flew squares where we were. Finally, the controller came on the speaker with some words that caught my attention. "You should be able to see a Delta 727 approaching from the east. You will be to his right and about 2,000 feet above. Line up behind him at your attitude. An Eastern Airlines flight has been cleared to take off when you get into that position. When the Eastern plane breaks through the clouds, this will give a good heading and position for the runway. The visibility is two miles. Follow the delta plane into the cloud and you should break through with enough altitude to land. Do you copy?"

"Roger," was our reply.

The details were discussed back and forth several more times between the ground and our plane, but we had a way down if we could manage it.

The pilot gave up looking for a repair and returned to his position in the seat flying the plane. I lost most of my apprehension and noticed things around the cockpit. The pilot's uniform coat was somewhere behind me on a seat where he had thrown it, his shirt was wet with sweat, his tie was loose, and his hat was nowhere to be found. He brushed his wet hair from his forehead and began to fly the plane.

The co-pilot was also wet on places on the back of his jacket. He had been busy flying and, on the radio, so he had not left his seat.

I must admit that I have reacted to the adrenaline which must have been released, for I was soaked and wet. Then, there was the fear I had felt, not so much of death, but more of the pain I was so certain would precede death. There were those thoughts of self-recrimination, *"Why had I willingly allowed myself to be placed in this compromised position by that pseudo-promise of business to come?"* I thought of my family, *"at least my company flight insurance would cover this, as this Witch Hazel's Broom was a scheduled airline."* and then I prayed. As I became more confident of the outcome and felt that most of the danger had passed, I couldn't help myself from looking out to the sky to try to spot the Delta plane. As you have guessed by now, we found the Delta plane, saw the Eastern Airlines plane, obtained the compass heading for the runway, found our way through the clouds, landed on the runway and arrived safely at our gate.

I caught the next flight into Atlanta and arrived home Wednesday night as I had planned. I had played it safe and phoned home from the New Orleans Airport giving my wife my latest flight arrangements so she shouldn't worry when I arrived a little later than I had originally planned. She reluctantly accepted this new time and I did my best to be there.

I never told my wife about either the results of the sales call or of the ride on Witch Hazel's Broom. I wondered if I told her of the futility of the trip if she would question more of my trips. If I told her about Witch Hazel's Broom, she might begin to worry every time I flew. So, that is why I have the enjoyable company of your presence on this drive.

One Chinaman

I was working in Chattanooga the day One Chinaman *bought the farm*. I had just completed a sales call at a foundry on Chestnut Street at W. 26th and had headed towards my car when I saw the black smoke coming from the 124 Freeway to the north of where I was standing. I headed for where my car was parked to get in and turn on my CB radio to try to find out what had happened. It was a beautiful clear spring day in 1976, which made the dark billowing smoke even feel more ominous.

This was during the time when the Federal Government mandated that the states set the highway speed limit at 55 miles per hour. Most truckers, most salesmen, and many ordinary people who used the roads used Citizens Band radios when they traveled. Most of us used the CB radios to find traffic backups and accident locations that could be avoided by changing our route, at least that was the stated intention.

The more common use was to warn other drivers of the location of the speed traps and to spot police traveling on the highway as we speed along, usually going faster than the 55-mile per hour speed limit. The police were usually referred to as Smokies as their hats were similar to those worn by Smokey the Bear in the popular forest fire adds. Those of us who regularly used the CB adopted CB names for anonymous.

These names were referred to as *"Handles"*. Some of the handles used around the south at that time were Daddy Rabbit, Hound Dog, Left Wheel, Bunny Snatcher, Big Dog and the like. My handle was the Ace of Diamonds. Many times, the truckers would all travel more or less together at speeds hovering around 70 miles an hour forming what they would call a convoy.

They would be talking back and forth on the CB with truckers coming at them on the other side of the road, wanting to know where the Smokies were traveling or set up to stop them for speeding. There was always one CB-er in the lead and this one would be referred to as "on the front door" or "as the front door". Many times, four-wheelers would join the convoy.

When I got to and in my car, I turned on the CB radio to inquire as to what the smoke on I24 was. The sound I heard was an ununderstandable garble of words. I adjusted the squelch on the radio and things became clearer. In the language spoken in CB lingo, a four-wheeler had done something stupid on the road. This caused the driver of an eighteen-wheeler to lose control, in an attempt to avoid hitting more four-wheelers. The result was that the cab of his truck went over the side of the bridge over US Highway 11. The cab of his truck was hanging over the side barrier on fire.

I sat there in stunned silence listening to the chatter, with my mic in hand ready to ask for more information, one of the drivers asked about the driver who went over the side of the bridge. Another driver chimed in with the information that the cab of the truck was hanging over the edge of the bridge and was on fire. Someone else chimed in that One Chinaman was driving that eighteen-wheeler.

I knew One Chinaman. He drove a cab over an eighteen-wheeler truck for Refrigerated Trucking Company. We had had coffee together one afternoon at a truck stop on I85 a couple of years ago. It was one of those times when I was coming home from a sales trip and in a hurry. I had joined the convoy somewhere in South Carolina and it ended up that, at this time, I was on the front door.

We had been talking together for several hours and they had assumed that I was in an eighteen-wheeler. I had just taken the front door from One Chinaman. He looked down from the window of his cab to see what, in his words was a little baby poop, yellow, foreign car with this long whip antenna taking his doors.

For the next hour, he and the other truckers kept us all awake with comments about the car, its size, the funny looking whip antenna, and me having the guts to drive it that fast. As we got closer to Atlanta, the drivers in our convoy invited me to join them at a truck stop for coffee. We had a good coffee break and they wanted to inspect that little car I drove. It was a VW Dasher, two-door coup with a full whip antenna mounted off the back bumper.

Over the next couple of years, every time I came upon a Refrigerated Truck Line eighteen-wheeler with the little penguin painted on the back doors, I would ask the driver if he knew One Chinaman. Many times, I would end up convoying with One Chinaman. He would always joke about my little baby poop, yellow four-wheeler.

My attention turned to what I was hearing on the CB radio. I24 was shut down, US 11 was shut down, and the report was that the Chattanooga Fire Department was on the scene trying to do something about the black smoke. I couldn't see anything of the accident from where I was parked, so I crossed through the traffic backed up on US 11 to Cowart Street, which was a dead end.

I could drive to the end of Cowart Street, and get a closer look at the wreck hanging over the edge of the bridge. There, I saw the tractor still connected to the trailer, but hanging precariously over the edge of bridge. The tires and the fiberglass cab were still burning, producing that dark black sooty cloud of smoke. The fire department was working from under the wreck trying to put out the blaze. There were fire trucks on I24, working their way toward the wreck through the lines of backed up cars and trucks.

I turned off the engine and sat in the car, my eyes riveted to the scene in front of me and listening to the descriptive chatter on the CB. I picked up the mic and said,

"KTZ 7509 on the air, Breaker, Breaker 19, The Ace of Diamonds calling, did the driver make it out of the cab? Over."

Alan M. Oberdeck

"Breaker for The Ace of Diamonds, no he didn't, O'l Blue said that, over."

"Thank you for the comeback O'l Blue, The Ace of Diamonds over and down." I sat there almost in shock and watched as the fire department started to get the fire under control. We, who were on the road so much, knew things like this could happen, but when they did, and we knew the driver, it was devastating. He was a friend from the road who had bought the farm, who I had talked to for two years, and I didn't even know his name.

Finally, I realized that there was nothing I could do. I said a prayer and gave a salute to my friend. I turned the car around and with a heavy heart, went to my next sales call. Things like that stay with you. You never really forget and even now when I drive over that bridge in Chattanooga, I remember that beautiful spring day in 1976.

Eine Coke bitte!

Many years ago, before traveling became so difficult, a group of us were coming back from a business meeting in Germany. We arrived at La Guardia later than expected and were further delayed in our trip through customs. While in Germany, I had purchased several items of clothing; a shirt, coat, and a German Fisherman's wool hat all of which I was wearing when we deplaned. During those days, as the travelers walked from the deplaning area, they had to pick up their luggage to go through Customs. At this point, they were separated into two groups, those who were U.S. Citizens would have their passports checked and be free to go, or their baggage would be forwarded to their destination. Those who were not U.S. citizens would have to pass through Immigration. I must have looked very German as they tried to have me go through Immigration. I had to show my passport early to be allowed into the correct line.

It took us quite a while to pass through customs and recheck our luggage to our destination. We then proceeded to the boarding gate for the flight to our home city. When we arrived at our boarding gate, it was about 8:40 in the evening. Most of us in our party were thirsty and wanted to purchase a Coke at the kiosk near our boarding gate.

Now, this was La Guardia Airport and things in New York aren't always as they seem. The sign posted on the kiosk listed the closing time as 9:00 p.m. Yet, when we approached the workers at the kiosk, they would not serve us. We were told that *they were already closing down*. Talk as we could, pointing out the published closing time and all, they still would not serve us. They informed us that they quit work at 9:00 and they cleaned up early so they could leave promptly at 9:00. The fact that our plane came in late and we were thirsty for a Coke was not of their concern.

The rest of our group huddled and discussed the situation, but I took a different approach. I reasoned that not all the kiosks would be closing early, so I went over to an adjoining concourse and tried to buy a Coke. It was now 8:40, and there I was also informed that they were closing and that there was no way I could get a Coke. I headed to another concourse. The time now was 8:50, as I approached the next kiosk. I was wearing my German hat, the coat, and shirt I had bought at Kaufhoff, so I figured that if the immigration people thought I was in the wrong line, I just might look foreign enough to get away with what I had in mind.

As I approached the counter I reached into my pocket and pulled out several one-dollar U.S. bills. Bills in hand, I stepped up to the kiosk and attracted the attention of one of the workers who was in the process of cleaning the counter.

I held up a one-dollar bill and stated, "eine Coke bitte."

The man at the counter ignored me.

I then held up two one-dollar bills and more loudly repeated, "eine Coke bitte."

"Go away, we are closed!" stated the man behind the counter as he looked away.

It was not 9:00 on the clock visible from the counter, so I pointed to the clock and the sign stating the business hours for the kiosk and in a demanding voice waving three one dollar bills repeated, "eine Coke bitte!"

Now I had attracted the other worker also and a small crowd. Both of the workers told me to go away.

I waved the dollar bills in my hand and in a demanding voice stated again,

"Eine Coke bitte!"

Stories Told by Traveling Salesmen

They each told me that they were closed in several different languages, but none in German so I persisted,

"Eine Coke bitte!"

This time one of the workers took my money and gave me 16 oz paper cup of Coke and the proper change. At 9:05, I bowed slightly to him and said, "Danke," and left.

With my cup of Coke in hand I walked back over to our boarding gate.

"Where did you get that?" one of the men in the group asked.

"I have vays!" I jokingly responded pronouncing ways with a German accent.

The Interview

It was the spring of the 1970 college school year. The company I worked for at that time needed to hire a sales trainee. Since my company was located in the Northern Mid-West, I chose to interview candidates graduating from the several mid-sized colleges located in the Mid-West.

It was the practice that the colleges set aside a few days at the end of the school year to invite interested companies to come in and interview the graduates for positions they needed to fill. The candidates to be interviewed for these positions were usually found in two ways. The school furnished a list of candidates with their major along with a short bio. The companies looked over the list and choose which ones they wanted to interview. Also, the school posted a list of the companies that were coming to the event. The interested graduates then choose which ones they were interested in interviewing with.

I chose this particular school as it was known for its Marketing, Accounting, and Management departments. It also was known for attracting many of the returning veterans from the war. This meant some of the graduates being older and more mature.

This was the 1970s, and many things had changed from when I had graduated in the 60s. There was this Vietnam War going on, and all of the demonstrations that that brought about. There was this great fear of the population explosion, and the popular pressure was to limit family size to two kids.

There were women seeking equality who were burning their bras. There was the assignation of Martin Luther King, which among other things, led to racial unrest in the big cities. There was the assignation of Robert Kennedy that was still remembered, and there was the hate of President Nixon. These were the background issues present that year. In the colleges, these were the things still being discussed.

There were also the more conservative attitudes of the Mid-West as compared to the more liberal attitudes of those living in the North-East. With this racial unrest in the big cities and this in the background, it was an interesting time to interview graduates. You never knew what attitudes you would find in the person you choose to interview.

At this college, the interviews all took place in the gym with little curtained cubicles containing a table and two chairs. These were set up all around the perimeter. For the sake of confidentiality, the booths assigned for each company and industry doing interviews were separated from their competitors by the booths of noncompeting companies and industries. This meant that those companies looking for Marketing prospects, as I was, were separated by the booths of those looking for other skills.

It so happened that the cubicle next to mine was occupied by an interviewer from the New York Accounting firm, Fixem, Shilling, Pence and Price. Him interviewing graduates from the Mid-West was a mystery to me, but on the other side of the curtain, there he was. During one of the breaks, out of pure curiosity, I introduced myself to Mr. Fixem.

I learned he was here to recruit Accountants from the Mid-West because his firm had some customers that had plants in the Mid-West. It seemed that the Accountants in his firm were having some difficulty serving the Mid-West clients. His answer to the problem, he thought, was he needed *to "solve the problem"* by getting some diversity in the firm. *"Some of their own kind"* was how he put it. Well, *a little snobbish*, I thought to myself as I walked away back to my own cubicle.

After meeting him though, I thought he surely led credence to the joke about accountants that was making the rounds among others that were there.

The joke went this way,

It seems that the owner of an accounting firm was interviewing Accounting graduates to add an Accountant to his staff. He had invited several prospects to his office. They were all sitting on chairs in the secretary's office waiting to be called into his office for the interview. Each went into his office, in his own turn, and they asked him three questions.

The first question was, what is your name?

The second question was, if I hire you, when could you start work?

The third question was, what is 2 + 2?

To the last question, the prospect usually answered 4 and was dismissed. This happened to all the candidates except one.

The last candidate went into the office and was asked his name.

"Bob Smith," he replied.

He was then asked when he could start,

"Immediately," he answered.

He was then asked for the answer for adding 2 + 2.

He thought for a moment then rapidly went over and locked the door. He then went to the windows and closed the drapes. He then went to the desk, leaned across the front of it, and whispered to the owner.

"How much do you want it to be?"

And he got the job. This joke exactly fit my impression of Bruce Fixem.

For me, the interviewing went quite well. I had already met several veterans that I was going to invite to our factory for further interviews. They were older men with the kind of military experience that should place them in an excellent position to sell our products. Picking among them would be difficult. I was getting ready to pack up and go when I heard what I thought would be an interesting conversation coming from the other side of the curtain. I didn't see the candidate, but the conversation caught my attention.

"Hello, I'm George Smith and I got your invitation to come to your booth for an interview," he said apprehensively.

I heard a chair sliding on the wood floor as Bruce was probably standing up from behind his table to shake George's hand.

"Welcome to Fixem, Schilling, Pence, and Price, I'm Bruce Fixem."

There was a pause as he was probably shaking George's hand.

"Have a chair and sitdown, George," Bruce said with his Northeast accent.

"Thank you," George answered.

I heard what had to be two chairs sliding on the floor being positioned across the table from each other as they both sat down.

"Here is a copy of my resume."

I assumed that George had handed it across the table to Bruce.

After a long silence Bruce said,

"I see here that you took the usual Accounting classes and you also took the extra classes on Auditing. Most Accounting students don't do that. What led you to do that?"

"Working with numbers comes easy for me. I had the extra time to fit the classes in, so I decided that knowing about Auditing might come in handy," he replied.

"Looking this over it looks like you got all As," Bruce replied sounding a little like this surprised him.

"Like I said, Accounting came easy to me. Actually, you could say working with the numbers is more like a game to me," George replied.

"Your grades do look pretty impressive," Bruce stated.

"We are looking for people who show aptitude and a desire to succeed."

After a long pause probably to look over the rest of the resume Bruce observed,

"I see you came here from the small town of _____ in Wisconsin. How do you like life in the big city?"

"Actually, the 'small town' wasn't that small. In fact, it is pretty close to a big city so nothing really changed," George answered.

The tone and inflection in his voice left me thinking that he was wondering where this man from New York learned his geography, because his small town was well known.

"So, if we were to make you an offer you wouldn't be overwhelmed by working in a big city like New York," Bruce stated in a droll somewhat dismissive manner.

"I think I could adapt," George stated in like manner.

By the manner of his reply he must have been thinking where does this guy get off?

"So, did you work your way through school or did your parents foot the bill?" Bruce asked in a more dismissive manner.

"I worked summers and worked around school and, what extra I needed, I covered with loans," George responded with what sounded like pride in his voice.

"You don't list any activities such as sports, clubs, or fraternities. Weren't you participating in the social activities associated with a well-rounded college experience?" Bruce quizzically asked.

"Actually, I was too busy studying and with my part-time jobs, to get involved with any of those activities. Those activities were more for the students who were there for the social aspects of a rounded college life. Those were the students who were there for a *'College Degree'* and had the money to spend. I knew what I wanted to do," George replied.

Now here is a guy after my own heart, I thought to myself.

"Well aren't you concerned about all of the problems in the world? The Vietnam War, the problems with cigarettes killing the people who smoke, or the population explosion, for instance? How are we going to feed the expanding world population in 20 years?" Bruce asked in an "I can't believe you aren't horrified by the prospect of the world starving" sounding voice.

"I haven't been involved in those kinds of movements. I just look at them as a fad," George answered, kind of in a manner to try to change the subject to something more relevant.

"You chose to go to school to become an Accountant, what does your father do for a living?" Bruce asked after what seemed to be a pause.

"My father is a farmer and he owns his own farm. Actually, one of my jobs during the summer to pay for my schooling was working around the farm, that and anything else I could pick up," George answered with what sounded like pride in his voice.

"Out of curiosity what does your father grow on his farm?" Bruce inquired.

"Well, he started out as a dairy farmer, but as the economy changed, he switched over to growing crops," George answered.

"What kind of crops does he grow?" Bruce asked.

"The big crop is corn with some oats and tobacco," George replied

"Tobacco!" Bruce exploded.

"Don't you know how damaging smoking is? How many people it kills? Do you know how many people die from cancer each year from smoking cigarettes? What kind of conscience do you have? You know how much damage the tobacco industry does to the people who smoke. How can you justify not confronting your father for growing it?"

George answered in a calm measured voice as if he had run out of patience with Bruce.

"Well, you were just pointing out to me about how the population explosion is out of control and that in 20 years people are going to starve! Well, my father raising his tobacco is doing something about it."

There was a long moment of silence.

"I can't wait until I tell this to my friends at the cocktail parties back in New York about this. They'll never believe this!" Bruce responded in an unbelieving voice.

"Thank you for the invitation," George said in a calm dismissive voice.

I heard his chair slide on the floor, and I assumed he was getting up to leave.

I marveled at how well George had handled that interview as I continued packing my things to leave. I wish he was interested in sales as I sure would have liked to interview him.

The Performance

He had been invited back to the home office to talk to them. *He* had been put out to pasture several years ago, but someone raised the question of how would he handle this? *His* company sold their product through distributors and now they were in trouble with one of the large ones.

He had been the best salesman the company had, gaining the territorial sales increases year after year, but at what cost? *He* never followed the programs the management planned; instead, *He* corrupted them to suit *His* own perception of what he called *the market*. And then, *He* committed the unpardonable sin of being successful while *He* did it.

In his early years, *He* kept offering suggestions as though *He* knew more about selling to distributors than the management. How arrogant! Later, *He* became more and more caustic with his suggestions, and to add insolence, kept up a mild stream of I told you so's as *His* suggestions were adopted by his competition. *His* reputation for success made it impossible to downright fire *Him*. Finally, *He* was given a small territory and ignored. Somehow, last year's sales meeting was scheduled during *His* vacation, and *He* was not encouraged to attend. Must have been a screw up in communications.

When the new Assistant Sales Manager had approached one of *His* large former distributors, some time ago and tried to get them to follow the prescribed company line, the crisis had begun. It wasn't a crisis for the distributor, they were happy to take their business to a competitor. The crisis was the loss of business for the company. That was why the President of the distributorship was sitting in the home office conference room for this meeting.

He had been tracked down in midweek as *He* worked *His* small territory and flown back to the plant for the meeting. One of *His* old friends from the Service Department had been assigned to meet *Him* at the airport and bring *Him* to the plant. None of the others wanted to be alone with *Him* for that long hour drive from the airport. *He* would ask too many pointed questions and argue with their answers. *He* could be a real obstinate pain at times. No one from management wanted to enter the meeting, exhausted from an hour of arguing with *Him* and after being told, "I told you so."

Eventually, *He* arrived. There, *He* stood, a gray tawdry embarrassment. He entered the room walking with *His* characteristic limp, *His* overweight body literally bulging out of *His* suit, *His* big belly protruding over *His* belt by at least five inches. *His* suit showing some wear, the fabric becoming shiny at the knees and elbows, the fabric being worn away on the corners of the flap on the coat sleeves at the wrist, and one coat sleeve had three buttons while the other had two. *His* limp tie just hung there with the short end occasionally appearing out from beneath as *He* moved. The white shirt appeared old. The collars and cuffs were worn-looking, almost threadbare, with little white pill balls showing whenever *He* moved *His* arms. *His* boots, as *He* never could be convinced to wear proper wingtip oxford shoes, looked polished on the toes as though *He* had rubbed them on something to make them shine, but the soles appeared worn. There were scuff marks on the heels and worn leather on the back of the boots. At least, these were zipper on the side boots and not cowboy boots. Cowboy boots would have been too much.

When *He* entered the room, the first thing *He* did was to go over and shake hands with the visitors. *He* didn't even address the management – right on to the visitors. *He* exchanged pleasantries with them, pulled out a chair across the table from them and began to take control of the meeting.

Stories Told by Traveling Salesmen

God knows why *He* was invited back, but it was supposed to be for show, to show a united front, not to take control of the meeting. And the chair, the chair *He* picked, that was left for the sales manager, and *He* took it.

He began the meeting for the second time. It didn't matter to *Him* that the Assistant Sales Manager that was *in charge* of *His* old account had spent the last hours outlining to the account how good the company was. How much work the company had done to put this program together, that had been presented, to them. Didn't *He* realize the strategy was to get the account excited about the "new" program and back on the band wagon.

He started the meeting by making a statement to the President of the account,

"I hear your purchases from us have gone way down and that you have begun to buy and resell our competitor's products. What happened?"

"Well, your company's product just hasn't been profitable for us lately and our salesmen sell what gives them the best commission," was the reply.

He pondered that for a moment and asked,

"When did this begin?"

"Shortly after you left the territory." was his answer.

They talked back and forth for a while, he, and the President of the account. The Assistant Sales Manager kept trying to salvage his agenda by interrupting to praise the merits of the new program, but each time his statements were ignored. It was obvious the Sales Manager was becoming disgusted by how *He* was treating the Assistant Sales Manager. After all, who was running this show after all.

Eventually, it became apparent that the President of the account was blaming the Assistant Sales Manager and his programs for the account's lack of ability to make their employees sell the company products. The accusation was that sales had dropped off a little more with each program change because the thrust of the programs served to benefit only the company at the expense of the salesman. This discussion continued until *He* asked the question that blew the last of the companies planned agenda away and changed the thrust of the meeting.

"What is it we can do to help?" *He* asked.

"How do you suggest we must act to help you build our business back?"

That opened the floodgates of Hell. All those possible suggestions, the implications, just imagine.

Ridiculous!

1. Wanting someone to visit the distributorship whenever they asked for help – Haven't they ever heard of a telephone?
2. Training their salespeople by going with them on routine sales calls – No one has time for that, management has more important things to do.
3. Modifying the program to provide larger distributor profits and salesperson's commissions – are they telling us how to run our business?
4. Wanting their phone requests answered within 24 hours – people here go home at night.
5. Etc.

He, that shabby old man, began to negotiate and make notes. *Him* and the President finally came up with a compromise program which to their way of thinking was advantageous to both parties. Then came the most arrogant thing *He* has ever done, *He* stands up, and walks over to the Assistant Sales Manager's chair and gives him the document that was agreed to by *Him* and the President of the account. *He* then said,

"Here is the agreement on what needs to be done to build back the company sales to this account. It's up to you to have this typed. Sign this agreement with the account, so you can begin to win the distributor's business back."

With that, *He* went over and shook the President's hand and announced that *He* had to leave to catch a plane. The President invited him to stop by soon to have a working lunch.

The Assistant Sales Manager gave a guarded sigh and went to prepare the pages that made up the agreement. The Sales Manager made a hasty exit to talk to *Him* before someone drove him to the Airport. His friend from the Service Department met *Him* in the hall ready to drive *Him* back to the airport.

The Sales Manager intercepted them. The friend from the Service Department watched as *He* left with the Sales Manager.

The assistant Sales Manager took care of the details and got the President of the account to the airport for his flight home.

The recap took place the next day. The Assistant Sales Manager met with the rest of us who had participated in the meeting. To put it bluntly, the Assistant Sales Manager was livid. *He* had usurped the authority, taken control, not followed the plan and to top it off, showed no respect when *He* came into the room. *He* should have sat in a chair along the wall and away from the table. *He* had to go. *He* would never set foot in the building again. The raving went on and on…

When the room became quiet, the Sales Manager rose from his chair at the end of the table and began to speak,

"Gentlemen, what you saw yesterday were two old-fashioned businessmen sitting down to make a deal the old fashion way. What you were seeing were the last vestiges of the past."

"Our company has adopted the modern ways to do business. *He* saved the account for us only because the account is old and backward. *He* won't be around to bother us anymore. *He* told me that the only reason he even answered the summons to come to the home office this time was that he felt duty-bound after all these years to try to protect an old account; an account that had given him good business for many years."

"He also came back to resign in person when he was done. Your troubles are over as *He* gave me his resignation on the way to the airport. *He* is history. And by the way, you probably should begin searching for new companies to put in place to replace that distributor when it becomes apparent that we really can't do business the old way anymore."

The Assistant Sales Manager arose from his chair and thanked the Sales Manager for the great news. He then announced that to celebrate the burying of the old and the advent of the new, he would buy a round of drinks at the local watering hole for all present after work.

The Sales Manager took me aside later and commented to me that it was hoped I had learned something from watching the old salesman work, because it was obvious that none of the other management had appreciated how *He* had been able to turn the situation around.

Will we ever learn?

Tom

I am not a cat person, but my wife is, therefore we have cats. One afternoon, about two years ago, a scruffy-looking gray, stray cat wondered onto our deck in search of food. We have two female cats, so we always leave a feeding container where they can get to it. They were away doing what they do to keep occupied. This cat found the dry food container and began to eat. Someone in the house made a little noise and this cat retreated with the greatest of frenzy from the deck.

A day or two later, this same cat appeared again at the dry food container. This time I decided to take a good look at it. The cat appeared to be a young cat, just older than what you would call a kitten. It had a small, cloth type collar, around its neck and its gray fur appeared matted and unkept. As the cat ate from the container, it kept looking around as if some predator was waiting to pounce upon it and it had to be ready to flee. I remained silent as I watched it eat as it appeared to be famished, and I didn't wish to scare it away as what had happened last time.

My wife was there near the window when the cat came back the next day to eat. Immediately, she moved silently to a place where she could get a better look at it. Her assessment, because of the collar, was that this cat had been someone's pet and it was either lost or had been abandoned. Her reaction was we should try to *help* it. We watched it eat and when it had eaten enough, it stealthily retreated from the deck. We did not see where it retreated to, but we concluded it had to be living close by.

Thus, began the slow process of trying to win the cat's confidence. First, we would wait until he would arrive and begin to eat, then we would make some little noise in the house. It would retreat around the corner, but when it sensed there was no danger, would return to the food. Then my wife began to talk to the cat in a soothing voice until it could accept that interruption while it was eating. Eventually, the time arrived when it would allow one of us to be out on the deck while it was eating. During this time, it was growing larger. Its fur began to look good and the collar around its neck was beginning to almost cause strangulation. One day, my wife was out on the deck when it came to eat and had a pair of scissors with her. She was able to catch the cat and cut the collar free. At that time, she also determined the cat was male and bestowed the name Tom upon him.

The female cats may have suspected he was coming to eat but were not guarding their food. Then came a time when all three cats were there at the same time. The two females, who hardly tolerated being at the same place together themselves, decided to join forces and attack Tom to defend their food. Tom made a hasty retreat and just learned how to avoid them.

The most interesting day arrived when my wife decided that all the cats needed to go to the vet. We have a carrying cage, so she first caught the two females and placed them in the cage. Then when Tom came to feed, she caught him too and he went into the cage with the two females. Surprisingly, they all arrived at the vet without a scratch, got their shots, and arrived back home in one piece.

Tom has grown into a very handsome cat. He has a very soft gray coat with highlights here and there. When he sits facing you with his two front feet planted side by side and his tale wrapped around himself to cover his front paws, he has a pair of slightly lighter chevron strips on each of his front legs that make him appear very regal. When he walks, he walks with dignity. He has finally accepted us and will on occasion even jump up on my wife's lap.

I think the last act of acceptance came a few weeks ago when Tom presented us with a dead baby squirrel and a dead small snake.

Pondering Time!

Since I have retired, I have *time* to ponder the wonders of the universe. It takes *time* to ponder anything, therefore, without a great number of responsibilities, I have the *time* to do this.

Of course, when I retired, the company I worked for had to give me some memento to remind me of the *time* I spent in their employment. The management, being less than creative, put their heads together and came up with the most appropriate and conventional thing they could think of. They gave me a nice gold-plated *TIME PIECE* with the *time* I worked there in years engraved on the back. At my retirement party, they tried to make it as exciting as possible and give me the *"TIME-of-my-life"*. Needless to say, at my age, by the *time* I got home that day, I was exhausted.

For the first few days of my retirement, I laid around the house occasionally checking the *time* on my new *time piece* and taking the *time* to watch whatever was on the learning channel on TV. After about four days, I concluded that what was on the Learning Channel was mostly what I already knew, and it turned out to be a waste of *time*. Even the movie channels didn't help me pass the *time*. Eventually, my wife emphatically suggested that it might be *time* for me to get off my posterior and do something constructive around the house.

I started to take the *time* to look around the kitchen for ways to improve the efficiency of how things were done there. This *time,* my wife's reaction bordered on being violent as she picked up the black cast iron frying pan and suggested that if I wished to avoid a large, flat spot on the top of my skull, I would leave her kitchen alone. In no *time* flat I was out of the kitchen and into a safer part of the house.

Using my *time* to help my wife around the house apparently was a bad idea. Still the question arose as to what I would now do with all this extra *time* that had been bestowed on me by the rite of retirement. If I now had to be careful about what suggestions I could make around the house, maybe I could build something.

My work bench in the garage looked to be a place to begin my new construction career. There, before me was an accumulation of odds and ends, tools, and assorted fasteners. Finally, I decided to take *time* to organize my tools so I could find what I needed when I needed it. I took the *time* to back the car out of the garage and began to unload the pile of things from the work bench to the garage floor; the *time* to sort was upon me. Things went from pile to pile and back again. I looked at the mess and decided it was nap *time* and headed into the house.

In the earlier cooler *time* of the next day, after hearing some disparaging remarks about the car being covered with dew out in the driveway, I ventured back into the garage and sorted the mess. Eventually, with my tools all at my grasp, I found some wood and it was *time* to build the proverbial bird house. The *time* flew by as I measured, sawed, adjusted, sawed again, nailed, pulled things apart, and nailed again. The *time* spent on this project was nearing about three hours, when the vice that was holding it slipped from the bench and on its way to the floor encountered my big toe, crushing it.

Because of the embarrassment, I didn't tell my wife and took the *time* to drive myself to the Emergency Room. The *time* spent in the Emergency Room was painful and boring. The x-ray showed the bones were broken, so the toe was wrapped, and I was given some pain medication with the instruction that I was not to drive. It seemed like it took a long *time* before my wife got to the emergency room to pick me up.

After a period of *time,* my toe healed, and it was *time* to store my newly acquired crutches in the closet. The garage is now a show piece of organized tools. I now ponder *time* and approach it with awe. While I am looking at my TIME PIECE, I have decided that it is bedtime.

www.ingramcontent.com/pod-product-compliance
Lightning Source LLC
LaVergne TN
LVHW011937070526
838202LV00054B/4696